I0650672

Jefferys Taylor

The Farm

A new and entertaining account of rural scences and pursuits, with the toils,

pleasures, and productions of farming.

Jefferys Taylor

The Farm
A new and entertaining account of rural scences and pursuits, with the toils, pleasures, and productions of farming.

ISBN/EAN: 9783337228026

Printed in Europe, USA, Canada, Australia, Japan

Cover: Foto ©Andreas Hilbeck / pixelio.de

More available books at **www.hansebooks.com**

THE FARM:

OR
A NEW AND ENTERTAINING ACCOUNT
OF
RURAL SCENES AND PURSUITS,

WITH THE
TOILS, PLEASURES, AND PRODUCTIONS
OF
FARMING.

FOR YOUNG READERS IN THE TOWN AND COUNTRY.

PHILADELPHIA:

J. B. LIPPINCOTT & CO.

1861.

CONTENTS.

INTRODUCTION.

I HAVE, at the moment of commencing the following little volume, two classes of readers in my view—the one belonging to the city; the other to the country. It is my design to benefit both.

But, pray, what interest can one born in the city, and who expects there to spend his days, have in farming operations? Let us see.

Perhaps you are one day to become a merchant, a manufacturer, a lawyer, or a judge, and you are to live in a fine house, either in Boston or New York, or some other large city, and you ask, what have *I* to do with farming?

Now, you have an interest in your country — have you not? You desire her prosperity? But that prosperity depends greatly upon the fact, whether the farmers flourish or not. Suppose you become a *merchant*. You build a large store, and import a great quantity of goods. You aim to sell to the farmers. But if *they* are not flourishing — if they cultivate their lands badly — if they are indolent — if they are unenlightened and ignorant — they will raise but small quantities of wheat and corn, and prepare but little beef and pork for market. In such a case, what will become of *your* interest? They cannot purchase your goods, for they have nothing with which to pay ; or if you trust them you will lose your debts. Thus, in either case, if the farmers flourish not, the merchants will not flourish. They may import sugar, and coffee, and tea, into the country, but it will turn to no profitable account, unless the farming interest flourishes.

Should you become a *manufacturer*, the same things hold true. You may erect large establishments—gather many skilful artisans—and produce large quantities of excellent and useful articles. But what are they all worth, if there are no purchasers? And how can there be purchasers, if the farmers of the land are poor? They are a large class of the community. And if they are unable to purchase, you will have but a small demand for your cottons, your carpets, your nails, your axes, and the like.

And besides, if the farming interest flags, as they say, who is to support the mechanics? Where will you obtain your wheat, your rye, your potatoes, your beef, your pork, and other necessaries, while you are carrying forward your manufacturing interests?

But perhaps you intend to become a *lawyer* or a *judge*. Well, these are honourable professions—but even then you will be dependent upon farmers. For if they bring nothing to market, all your learning will not produce for you one loaf of bread, or serve up on your tables one roast turkey.

You perceive then, city-born, and city-bred, as you may be, you have an interest in the prosperity of the farmers of the land. All other professions in life are dependent upon this class of the community. Stop the cultivation of the soil, and we could have no commerce and no manufactures—we could have no large towns, nor splendid cities.

People of the city are sometimes wont to look down upon those of the country. This is wrong. The profession of agriculture is most honourable and important. You may gather, from what I have said, somewhat of the dependence of all classes upon farmers.

And hence you may learn the importance of knowing something about farming. The more you are acquainted with the subject, the more just sentiments you will entertain of its importance—of 'its pleasures—of its perplexities. You will perceive the justice of giving to the farmer a *good price* for what has cost him so much toil. You will encourage him by every means in your power, and on a wet day, or a cold morning in January, when he has come some ten or a dozen miles to bring you the rich productions of his land, you will not be so much disposed to get a *"good bargain"* at *his expense.*

Besides, with some knowledge of farming you will be better able to judge of the *qualities* of the products which are brought to market.

Farmers generally know more than others by inspection about the fine or poor qualities of wheat and rye—of corn and potatoes. And such knowledge would be valuable to you, in almost any department of life, especially if you should one day have a family, and need to purchase the materials of living for them.

And lastly, I would set forth to my city readers the value of some acquaintance with farming on the score of *pleasure*. You sometimes make excursions into the country. What a gratification to be able to make the distinction between good and bad husbandry! What a source of pleasure to be able to pronounce, in any given case, whether a farm is well taken care of—to determine whether a field is well ploughed!—or well mowed!—or well reaped! —to decide as to the good or bad qualities of the horses, or cattle, or sheep, or swine, which you notice as you pass along.

Some knowledge on these points you may obtain without spending an apprenticeship to farming. You may learn much from books. And it is one design of this little volume to impart some just ideas on the subject for your benefit.

But I write for another class also. I expect a portion of my readers belong to the country. They are the young farmers of the land—the bones and sinews of society—coming forward rapidly, and every thing will soon depend upon them.

I need not dwell long on the importance to this class of a thorough knowledge of farming. I might with as much propriety talk of skill to the tailor in handling his sheers and his needle. Every one knows this. And many farmers know that without a thorough acquaintance with their business, they are liable to make poor crops and "to come out at the little end of the horn," as the saying is.

But leaving so plain a point as this, I would say a few words to my young friends in the country on the dignity and independence of their employment.

The life of a farmer is indeed employed about the earth. But it is no mean concern. Cincinnatus was a farmer. Washington was a farmer. And in older times Abraham cultivated flocks and herds—and David, who in after years sat upon the throne of Israel, was himself a shepherd. No man in society is so independent as the farmer. He lives more entirely within himself than any other class. He raises the necessaries, and not a few of the comforts and luxuries of life. Nor is any profession more dignified, or more removed from temptations to pride and vice.

What a delightful spot in this world of briers and thorns is the habitation, with its surrounding acres, of an honest, industrious, thrifty farmer! What an air of neatness and comfort all things wear! Even the grass seems to look greener than elsewhere — the shrubbery, all weeded out, smiles forth in the beauty of its flowers — the well trimmed trees put forth a richer foliage — the cattle seem to feel their superiority — the lambs skip somewhat more gaily, and even chanticleer raises his clarion voice some notes higher.

I love to dwell on such a scene; and I would wish to inspire my little readers in the country with contentment with their allotment. They are among the most happy, honored, and blessed of this world. At least they may easily become so. And although the business of farming is sometimes depressed, and is always a slow mode of gaining wealth; yet it is a far more sure method than by means of trade, in which every thing almost is fluctuating and insecure. A merchant's goods may easily be consumed, and his debtors may fail to pay him his honest dues. But the acres of the farmer are fire-proof and fast anchored. If he possesses but little, that little is comparatively sure. The man of wealth in the city, who rides in his coach to-day, may not even have a wagon to ride in to-morrow. But the farmer generally has this latter vehicle, at all times.

One thing farther, before I conclude this introduction. This little volume, to which I introduce my readers, is principally the work of an English author. It tells much about English husbandry. I have introduced into it some account of husbandry in the United States. I was the more willing to avail myself of the advantages of this work, as it will serve to give some just notions of the English style of farming, which in some respects is superior to our own, especially as to neatness and order. Englishmen, who visit us, are sometimes disgusted with the appearance of our farms and our villages, for in their own land they are accustomed to see them adorned by the hand of system and taste.

Let my little readers rivet well this matter in their minds. Should they ever become farmers, let them not forget that neatness and order are among the cardinal virtues of a good farmer. Without them, he cannot prosper, nor will his house and home be long pleasant to him. Besides, these are important in point of moral influence. Persons who are neat and attentive to method are more likely to be good, than the slovenly and the careless. Fix well then in your minds the old maxim, for it is worth a thousand times more than its weight of gold, "Have a place for every thing, and keep every thing in its place."

I shall conclude my introduction with some useful lines, which I think it would be well for every young farmer to learn—and every old farmer to practise :—

> Let order o'er your time preside,
> And method all your business guide.
> One thing at once, be still begun,
> Contrived, resolved, pursued, and done;
> Ne'er till to-morrow's light delay,
> What might as well be done to-day.
> Neat be your barns, your houses neat,
> Your doors be clean : your court-yards sweet;
> Neat be your barns; 'tis long confessed,
> The *neatest* farmers are the best.

THE FARM-HOUSE.

I SHALL begin by presenting to my readers a view of a farm-house, and as I happen to have only an engraving of an English one, I shall present them with that. See the frontispiece.

The name of the house is Peak Hall, or as the country people in England usually call it, "*Gable-sides.*" It was formerly the residence of a wealthy lord in Essex, in which county it is situated. It was not originally designed for a farm-house. Yet it is now the delightful residence of a thrifty English farmer, who has some four hundred acres of excellent land about him, and who cultivates it in the neat and excellent manner of the English farmer. The house obtained not either of those names without a cause; for its roof-peaks, or gable-ends, are no fewer than twelve in number. Three of them form the roof on one side; two on another; three at the back. Two projections for staircases have each a gable; and the very roomy porch in front has two. The building is all of red brick, and exhibits in front some curious sculptured ornaments in that material. The windows are of diamond quarry glass, and, like those of churches, have strong stone mullions, or partitions, instead of wooden frames. The ivy on the further side has crept unmolested nearly to the garret windows; and hangs nodding from the porch-roof in a very picturesque manner. Two enormous six-columned chimneys stand twenty-five feet higher than the ridge tiles, and give a sort of dignity to the building. The front door is six feet wide, seven feet high, and nearly three inches thick. It is studded with eight hundred and nine iron knobs; it has an iron grating, about six inches square, through which to parley with strangers after night-fall; and it swings on hinges, reaching the whole width of the door. The sides of the porch have twisted spiral balusters, through which to look, without going from under shelter.

It must not be imagined that the front of this ancient dwelling, pretty and remarkable as it is, can be seen completely from the road leading nearest to it. The farming buildings, as is common in some parts of England, stand nearly before it. The long barn and cow-sheds, if they did not stand on rather lower ground, would hide the house altogether. The frontispiece gives as good a view as can be taken, and is from a spot at a short distance from the bridge.

C

As in farming we have a good deal to do with *acres*, I may as well state here, that four thousand eight hundred and forty square yards make one square acre, and that each side of that space will therefore be about sixty-nine yards and a half long. Each acre contains four roods, each rood forty poles, and each pole rather more than thirty yards. Our farm-yard occupies, with the various buildings, about five roods, or an acre and a quarter. The buildings are principally these:—two great barns; stables; two granaries; hay-barns, cow-houses, piggeries, hen-houses, pigeon-houses, and a cottage for our head man and his family; though this scarcely stands in the yard. There is a railed partition, forming, with the hedges, an inclosure, called the *rick-yard*. In this part stand now four stacks of hay, containing, together, about two hundred loads; five stacks

PEAK HILL FARM.

of wheat-corn; two of clover-hay; a bean-stack or two; a fagot-stack; and a tolerably large one of straw. Towards the north the cattle yard is fenced by a haulm, or stubble-wall, which has lasted, and is likely to continue several years.

I must now describe a little more particularly the buildings. First, the barns. These, on the usual plan, are oblong structures. The largest is nearly sixty feet in length, and about thirty-five feet wide. This space is divided into three parts: the middle, reaching across the barn, from door to door, is called *the floor;* being laid with stout and smooth oak boards,—so smooth, as most boys know they usually are, that a good slide may be had upon them; —and *a bad* one, if a projecting nail catch the foot, and cause an unlucky fall. This part, on which wagons enter to deposit their loads, pass-

ing out at the opposite doors, is separated from
the sides, called *bays*, by planks or rails, a few
feet high. In the bays the corn is stacked,
ready for threshing. A small granary is inclos-
ed in one corner of this barn.

As to the principal granary, I remember
trying to shew my wisdom once, by saying that
it was nonsense to set it upon legs, and make
men ascend with heavy sacks on step-ladders.
The twelve stone pillars on which it stands
have each a projecting cap, like a mushroom
top; at which I also laughed, as being utterly
useless, till my uncle told me he thought *I had
a mushroom top*, not to know that granaries
were so built to keep a floor free from wet;
and that the pillars were capped to prevent
rats and mice from climbing into the place,
where they would be glad enough to obtain
board and lodging. The granary has sun-

dry bins or partitions for various grain and seeds.

The stables have stalls for fourteen horses, including two of better quality for our own riding nags. I need say nothing about racks and hay-lofts, which are equally common in town or country.

The hay-barns are like roofs of houses set on very tall legs, with opening weather-boards extending part of the way down, something like those of a brew-house. Hay, stacked therein, of course requires no thatching; but I always think that is the sweetest which stands in the open air.

The cow-houses consist of a long range of sheds, for milking principally, and for nursing the calves. These have stalls, with moveable frames of wood, made to receive the head of the cow, and detain it, lest the animal should

turn and throw down the milk, or otherwise
interrupt the process. Piggeries and dove-
cotes need not be described, as they may be
seen in other situations. The brew-house and
bake-house join the dwelling.

I have ranged the farm-yard with my note-
book in my hand, and can find nothing more to
detain us at present, unless it be to notice some
large wooden frames, which are used as cow-
cribs, to contain winter fodder for cattle.

In the mean time I will ascend a rising
ground, whence the greater part of the farm
can be surveyed. Our four hundred acres consist of about thirty-five inclosures, divided, as
is common in this country, and other wood-
land parts, by ditches and hedge-rows, gar-
nished with the varied forms of stately timber
and flowery leafy shrubs. Of those inclosures
twenty-one are arable, or plough-land, amount-

ing to about three hundred acres out of the four hundred. The rest is pasture, meadow, wood, or waste, including roads and paths.

Most fields belonging to every large farm in the United States have names, by which they are designated; such as the *mill-lot, shop-lot,* &c. These are generally derived from some peculiarities of shape, soil, or situation. Some from accidents, or incidents of life and husbandry. A few are difficult to account for: but as our country has been recently settled, the origin of most of our farm-lot names is well known. But in England, it is otherwise. In that country particular lots are more commonly named than with us: yet the occasion of their names has been extensively lost. The farm of *Gable-sides,* some account of which has been given, presents a curious specimen of the manner in which lots are named in England. On this farm we read of *Fore Field; Back Field; Twenty Acres; Bridge Field; Bushy Croft; Little Bushy Croft; Mill Hoppet; Acre Piece; Flamsted Meads; Stony Field; Path Field; Pond Field; Little Go; Wood Side; Parish Field; Brook Field; Topsey Wood; Long Mead; Shoulder-of-Mutton Field; Great Hide; Little Hide; May Field; Pig's-Mutton Field; New Slip; Pole-hurst Side; Steeple Land; Steward's Corner; Eleigh Plot; Five Farthing Close; Abbot's Bury; Oak Field; Hatch Field; Lane Field; Peak End; Downshire Bottom.*

These are the well-known inclosures and plots of Gable-sides Farm. A word of explanation with regard to a term or two in the list will be important. *A hoppet* is in Essex, and some other parts of England, a small piece of ground, usually near the house, elsewhere called a *paddock*. *Flamsted* [formed of *sted*, Saxon for *a place*, and *flam* or *flame*,] indicates the situation of some village conflagration, of which the tradition still remains. *Little Go* is merely a short cut, or track-way, into the high road, passable only in summer. *Great Hide* and *Little Hide* :—the word *hide* was much used formerly for a plot or parcel of land; because measuring thongs were cut from the hide of a bullock, and as much as one skin, thus lengthened out, would inclose, was called "*a hide of land.*" In the days of William the Conqueror, this phrase was used for a hundred acres. As to *Pig's-Mutton Field*, the story is merely this, that a sheep, many years ago, was killed there, and nearly devoured by a ravenous sow; but I rather doubt the tale. *Pole-hurst Side* reminds us of a neighbouring copse, or thicket; *hurst*, or rather *hyrst*, being the old Saxon word for a grove. *Steeple Land* is a roundish knoll, of some height, from which spot the distant spire of Danbury Church can be occasionally seen. *Abbot's Bury* refers to some dwelling, or spot, connected with an abbot's history;—*bury* meaning simply a residence. Lastly, *Downshire Bottom* is a low marshy field, near the brook. The word *shire*, from the Saxon verb, which means *to divide*, is seldom used but for the great partitions of the kingdom into counties. Sometimes, however, as in the case of the Gable-sides Farm, it has an application, of smaller importance, to the situation of a particular estate.

TILLAGE.

WE find, that, even in Paradise, man had employment appointed him; the object of which was, to aid nature in the production of food for his subsistence. It is true, that the varieties of the earth's provision were designed by the Almighty, without any of our contrivance, and that these have always grown in a way that the understanding of man has not been able even to comprehend. But, ignorant as we are, and vain as would be our attempt to interfere with the *designing part* of creation, we can do much by observation, and the exercise of our reasoning and bodily powers: marking what circumstances of an external kind have an influence upon these things;—what is favourable, and what injurious; so that skill and labour may arrange matters to improve the desired result. God entrusts the fitful gales of heaven to scatter innumerable seeds, which are to produce food or shelter for myriads of inferiour animals, or to deck the wilderness with flowers. But he employs a more regular and important agency, for the spread and cultivation of those plants which are especially destined for the support of man, and of those creatures which subserve his wants;—even the mind and hand of the great consumer, man himself. It is not presumption to say that man assists the purposes of nature, any more than to affirm that the motions of the elements may do the same. The Creator appoints and employs the instrument, whatever it be, whether an intelligent or inanimate machine; and we may, therefore, as truly admire his work and wisdom in the fruits of human art and labour, as in any of those natural wonders, in the formation of which the busy brain and finger of our race have had nothing at all to do.

Things are so ordered, excepting in a very few spots of the globe, that nature performs but little for man, unless man, in his turn, perform something for nature. She gives an abundance of materials and inducements, and then says, "Work! Work!" If, instead of obeying this reasonable injunction, we merely reach forth an indolent hand to receive her bounties, she usually bestows them in diminishing and inferiour portions, until, at length, our very necessities are unsupplied. In few countries, unless, indeed, within the tropical climates, the inhabitants scarcely exist a year on the mere donations of the soil and of the skies. It is as true, that the great mass of the people throughout the globe *must work*, as that they *must eat*. They must ply well their brains and their hands, or the table even of the cottager will lose its plainest viands. Persons brought up in cities, are too apt to think that grass and corn, beef and mutton, grow as matters of course; and that the countryman has nothing to do but to cut and eat. I hope to be able, before I have done, to shew my young friends that this is quite a mistake.

We will now take a little notice of those processes of moving the soil, which constitute the art of tillage.

The plough is, and has been, the grand implement of husbandry for this purpose, amongst all civilized nations. The form and power have varied much, as they now do in different counries; but the intent and general result have .een the same as far back as the ancient coins of Greece and Rome take us, many of which represent this noted agricultural machine, drawn by cattle and guided by a man, as now.

We cannot go farther into the history of the plough at present. As it was found, that the more the soil is loosened, stirred, and broken, the greater are its powers of production; it became needful to contrive some means of performing this operation on a large scale, in the most expeditious and successful manner. Spade husbandry, as it is called, does as well, perhaps better, where it can be accomplished; but millions of acres cannot thus be tilled.

In order, therefore, to move as much soil in as little time as possible, the plough was constructed. It consists of many parts; as the *coulter*, the *share* and *breast*, the *handles, rail, chains*, &c. The *plough-share* and *breast*, which are the principal acting parts in turning over the soil, consist of a broad and smooth surface of iron, having a sharp and taper toe, which enters, like a wedge, and heaves the earth off towards the right side. The *coulter* is a sort of knife, which is placed before the share, to cut the ground and detach the portion ready for it there. The engraving represents one of the common sort.

D

The terms *"ploughman"* and *"clod-hopper"* are used in a sneering and vulgar way, by many who do not possess nearly the skill and knowledge of the humble peasant who guides this important machine. In the first place, the parts of it are by him adjusted to a very great nicety, with screws, hooks, and wedges, according to the kind of furrow required;—and then the direction of this. in straight and parallel courses; the management, by the voice, of the horses—although a boy helps to guide them ; the turning and returning correctly; and the arranging of the furrows in slightly rising curves, or *länds*, as they are sometimes called, to lay them dry, with water-courses between; —all these duties require the ploughman to have a correct eye, a strong and steady hand, and · a clear head for his business—which qualifications make a man of a sort that

none but extremely ignorant persons can de-
spise.

Ploughing is often repeated, in various ways
before the land is sufficiently stirred and broken
to make a good *tilth*. For this purpose, the
field is, sometimes, crossed and re-crossed, in
different directions; but if not, the ends of the
furrows must be made good by a few cross
furrows, called *head-lands*. But, after all the
plough can do, the clods are still by far too
rough and large to receive the seed until
another engine has been employed.

This is the HARROW, a strong and heavy frame of wood, having a number of iron spikes fixed in it, to form a kind of rake for the surface. In the United States, the wedge harrow is chiefly used. It is so called from its being shaped much like a wedge. In England, the square harrow, like that represented in the cut, is mostly used. The latter are now not unfrequent among us. In this country, we generally use but one, which is drawn by oxen; but in England three or four of these are frequently chained together, and drawn by two or more horses; they produce a great effect in cutting, crumbling, and levelling the clods, which are also, in some cases, further broken down by the action of a ponderous wooden roller.

But the utmost skill in the performance of these mechanical processes will not ensure a good return, unless the master's management be also good. As the husbandman needs food and rest, so does the soil, where the kind of produce called *a crop* is expected. The food of land is MANURE; its rest is laying it down either for feeding, or A FALLOW.

Manure consists of various animal, vegetable, and mineral substances, selected according to the soil and the intended crop. With respect to animals, there is no part of them which does

not, by dissolution, become a most useful ingre-
dient for the restoration of an exhausted soil.
Besides, therefore, the commonest kind of
manure, any refuse of the butcher and the
fishmonger, the soap-maker and the sugar-
boiler, is acceptable to the farmer;—who, of
course, has in this respect an advantage, if at
no great distance from places where these are
to be procured.

Lime, salt, burnt earth, sand and shells, soap-
ashes, and I know not how many other things,
with decayed vegetable matter, are applied to
the earth, as a sort of re-payment, for which,
however, she always accounts with high interest.
Meadows pay well for the best manure, but will
be mended much, even by more earth sprinkled
on the sward.

There are many other things essential to
good tillage, which the experienced and intelli-

gent farmer attends to, as he sees occasion; I shall mention only *weeding*, or *cleaning* the land, and *land-ditching*. The best opportunity for getting the field clear of weeds, roots, and other such matters, is afforded by the fallow. The ground is then at liberty to admit of continued ploughings; and of thistle and dock-irons, or bush-hooks, to eradicate those troublesome intruders, for which they are intended; and, if necessary, of the shovel and mattock, to remove suckers and roots of trees. Weeding, however, goes on to a great extent with the hoe and other instruments, as we have seen, when the crops are up.

Land-ditching, or draining on certain humid soils, is almost as necessary as any other act of husbandry; indeed, without this, in many cases, all other tillage would be labour in vain. Where water hangs in the land, on or near the surface,

very long together, it checks the vegetation of
farming crops, so as to compel the husbandman
to adopt a remedy. This remedy consists in
draining. Drains are of various kinds. In the
United States we use chiefly open drains. But
in England, where the farmers are peculiarly
nice, and wish to make the most of the land,
both as to appearance and produce, they employ covered drains, or gutters, sometimes called in that country *thoroughs*. These are
generally from eighteen to twenty-four inches
in depth, thrown across the land in such directions as shall best suit the discharge of the
water to the ditches at the borders of the field.
When this is done, bushes are thrust in, and on
them a close covering of straw is placed. On
this the earth may be securely laid. A hollow,
sufficient for the water-passage, is thereby obtained, and no indications of the work are visi-

ble above, except the superiour fertility of the spot, which, indeed, is sometimes distinctly to be traced in lines corresponding to the drains beneath. By this means the beauty of the field is preserved, besides that no land is wasted.

Meadows and pasture land do not of course require, or admit, of the labour of arable fields. Nevertheless, they need attention; and if the land be at all good, they fully repay it. Grass lands, like others, will, in a short time, be overrun with weeds and suckers from trees, if neglected. Instruments are invented, therefore, as we have seen, to delve these out; and the more diligently they are used the better; for even the grass is rendered more vigorous by the movement of the soil thus occasioned. The herbage also needs renewal sometimes, by having fresh hay-seeds, &c. scattered over it.

I have said that meadows want good manuring: this is usually done in. frosty weather, when the heavy cart does not cut the sward. After this supply has been spread by the fork, the stones, shells, and other rubbish, which may have been brought on, are carefully picked up and removed. Soon after, the field should be *bush-harrowed,* with a machine formed of bundles of thorny shrubs, attached to a heavy wooden frame, which, being drawn up and down by a horse, combs and scratches the manure and loose earth about. Then comes the roller—a huge cylinder of wood, made to turn and support a timber frame of great weight, which sometimes is further increased by laying upon it a heavy piece of timber, a wagon-wheel, or some such ponderous body. This machine presses the earth and roots close, and levels many little hillocks which would otherwise encounter the mower's scythe, and take off its edge.

During the winter season, farmers in the United States employ themselves in a variety of useful ways, such as mending broken implements; threshing and carrying their produce to market; and in laying in a sufficient stock of wood, for the year. This generally occupies much time, and is among the most laborious services to which they are called.

In England the farmers have the advantage in being able to carry on a still greater variety of operations, by reason of the superiour mildness of the climate. They repair hedges and ditches, and clear lands of stumps, roots, and the like; which we are prevented doing unless at particular seasons.

I have spoken of the *hedges* of England. In this country we know little of *this* mode of enclosing our fields—our method being either with rails or stone. But in that country they make extensive use of hedges and ditches. Some account of this mode of dividing enclosures in that country will be interesting and instructive.

Several different shrubs and trees are made use of for hedges, such as the white-thorn, black-thorn, furze, holly, &c. But the white-thorn is the most proper for fences, as it grows quickly, is very durable, and makes a handsome appearance. In Germany, the farmers make use of a tree called the horn-beam. In the United States some attempts have been made to form hedges. Mr. Quincy, near Boston, several years since, set out ten thousand of the American Hedge-Thorn, which he obtained from Virginia. But they have not flourished well, nor are they found so well adapted to the purpose of hedges, as the English White-Thorn, of which I have spoken.

The manner of forming a hedge and ditch by the English farmer is as follows:—First, the ground is carefully marked out, and a line stretched along it, to guide the digger. Next, he pares off the turf, if any, and rolls it on one side. Then he proceeds to remove the earth, to the width, perhaps, of about five feet at top, and slopes the sides down to the depth, it may be, of three feet, with a bottom of one foot wide, throwing the soil up on one side, ready to be formed into the bank. If the purpose be merely to divide land occupied by the same person, it may not signify on which side the embankment is made. But if it is to be a partition between, say my estate and my neighbour's, I must not, of course, intrude upon his ground at all, either for hedge or ditch. The boundary line therefore between us, I must make the further side of my ditch; the earth I must lay on my own ground; so that hedge and ditch both belong to me.

Good workmanship is very conspicuous in hedging and ditching performed by a competent hand. The sides, edges, and bottom, are expected to be as true to their proper form as if wrought in a brick-mould. If they are not so, the water hangs, where it ought to run, the bank crumbles down, and the employer very justly complains. The bank is planted with young hedge-shrubs, or sown with furze or broom, or else furnished with a dead fence of bushes stuck in and wattled together.

Old hedges are much improved by thinning, topping, and *laying*. A quantity of the old wood is taken out. The younger branches are then chopped *nearly* off, close to the root, taking care always to leave a small width of the living bark. The branches are then laid down *almost* horizontally, and tied to stakes, or to each other. The consequence is, those branches, instead of growing, as before, to an useless height and scanty at bottom, send forth a multitude of snoots, which thicken the lower part of the hedge; nor does the wound inflicted by the hedge-hook make any material difference in the growth, after the first season.

The hedges which we have thus described, when flourishing, present a beautiful appearance, and add much to the rural aspect of the country. They are generally accompanied by a ditch, the hedge alone, especially when young, being insufficient to turn cattle. In the fox-chase, or in deer hunting, of which the English are remarkably fond, it often becomes necessary to leap these hedges and ditches The horses called "hunters" are trained to this service, and often become surprisingly skilful in passing them. Yet, it is always accompanied with danger both to rider and horse, and sad and even fatal accidents sometimes occur. A pleasant allusion is made to this kind of leap in the celebrated story of Monsieur Tonson, which is no doubt quite familiar to most of our little readers.

> "If e'er a pleasant mischief sprung to view,
> At once o'er *hedge and ditch* away he flew,
> Nor left the game till he had ran it down."

The winter, in England, is a convenient time also to mend roads, public and private; but in the United States this is generally done in the summer and autumn. Both in this country and that, the farmer is allowed, instead of paying money for that purpose, to employ his ?am n l carts for the repair of those roads in his parish which are not provided for by toll-gates.

Winter, though not the season, generally, for military enterprise, is not a bad time for the farmer to proceed against very many of *his* enemies, with any advantages of arms, engines, and generalship, which he may possess. The enemies which I now refer to, are rats, mice, and weasels; many kinds of birds and insects; and last, but not least in mischievous importance, many tribes of four-footed game! With regard to all these, no qualification for killing them is needful, but the power of catching or finding them; and for this purpose, various schemes and arts, and clever ones too, are made use of. In the United States much less attention is paid to the destruction of such creatures as prey upon and injure our crops, than in England. In this latter country rat-catching and mole-catching are professions by themselves, which are useful to the community as many of higher reputation. As moles burrow and pass in long subterranean passages, but near the surface, the catcher inserts, in the trackway of the little miner, a spring trap, the catch of which is attached to a strong stick, thrust in the ground, and bent down with force, so as to rise and pull violently a string to which the under-ground snare is attached. The animal in passing, is thus noosed and choked without the possibility of escape. The mole-catcher has two-pence or three-pence a-piece for every mole he destroys.

Rats and mice are destroyed in various ways, and to a great extent, by dogs, and cats, and owls, which are more useful in a farm-yard, than many persons who are paid in money to do their work. Otherwise they are taken by traps and snares, or destroyed by poison. They are, however, rarely got rid of entirely, when even all these methods are continually adopted. The other animals of the mischievous sorts are destroyed by the gun, when seen.

PRODUCE OF THE FARM.

WE have taken a little notice of the farm, and the husbandman's needful labours upon it, before he can enjoy the fruits. Let us now see what those products are; how he gathers them in, and disposes of them for his benefit.

It is evident that these things consist of varieties of the vegetable or animal kingdoms of nature. We will attend to vegetables first, for they were man's first food, and occupied his earliest agricultural thoughts.

The vegetables chiefly cultivated in the United States, for the food or use of man, are of three principal kinds:—grain, or seeds;

roots; and the herbs whose *substance* chiefly is used for food or manufacture.

In the first class, I include the principal species of grain or corn, as the English people call all kinds of grain, and some other seeds: as wheat, oats, barley, rye, peas, beans, tares, &c. In the second division, we have potatoes, turnips, parsnips, carrots, and mangel-wurtzel. In the third class, we must put the species of grass, clover, and other pasture plants; together with hops, hemp, flax, teasels, &c.

Now I do not pretend to say that my list, or arrangement, will include, by any means, *all* the plants which may be found on farm lands: indeed I could easily add many others which I can call to mind; but they are not grown in quantity, or for purposes of nearly equal importance with those I have named; and are, perhaps, in many cases, only sown by way of experiment.

Neither must it be thought that all the plants and products which I have named and describ-ed, are grown on every farm. Some lands grow no barley, potatoes, or turnips; and I scarcely ever knew a farmer who attempted al. in one season.

WHEAT.—This, to the civilized world at least, is the first, in importance and value, of all grain. There are several sorts; but I do not see that I have room and opportunity to distin-guish them much in this little book. So I shall only say, that we farmers talk chiefly of white, red, and spring wheat.

I dare say if man had been employed to contrive or invent a seed, or fruit, for the chief support of his race, he would have made it nearer in size to a quartern loaf, than is the diminutive grain of corn, which Nature has thought the best form and bulk for the purpose.

SPRING WHEAT. COMMON WHEAT.

Of this kernel, or corn, a considerable part is husk, which adheres so closely, that it is needful to bruise the whole together, and sift

out the meal, to separate it. Yet there is
"bread enough, and to spare," as far as *quantity* is concerned, wherever the wickedness,
the folly, or the indolence of man, does not
defeat or check the powers of nature, and of
his own skill and industry. It is a remarkable
fact, and one which ought to impress us with
sentiments of admiration and gratitude towards
the great and good Author of Nature, that
wheat, the best of grain, will grow and thrive
in almost any climate where vegetables constitute the food of man. From the equator to
the very borders of the polar regions, this constant friend endures the scorching beams, or
braves the northern blasts, and comes, a golden
gift, alike to the sun-burnt fainting African, and
the snow-wrapt Muscovite. Seeing that it
bears such extremes of climate, spreading from
zone to zone on the globe, it is not wonderful

that it sustains better than any other corn the
inclemencies of our own changeful skies, and
the disadvantages of our most unfavourable
seasons. Wheat may be compared to a very
sensible person, who likes and enjoys good
things as well as any one, but can put up with
bad circumstances better than most other persons. It thrives in a temperate climate, a fine
shining season, a rich soil, and under good
management; yet, when all these are reversed,
so that other things perish, this hardy plant will
live, produce its seed, and supply, in some
measure, the table of even the least worthy
husbandman.

Wheat, for the main crops, is always sown in
the autumn, and generally on land which has
been a *fallow* the preceding season, or which
has produced some different crop, and been
well manured. It was the general practice of

5 F

the ancients, and has been of the moderns, to
steep the seed in liquors of a briny kind, before
sowing; some, however, think that water alone

BUCK WHEAT.

is just as good; the benefit being rather, by the
means of a fluid, to separate faulty seeds, which
swim at the top, and are easily skimmed off,

than to impart additional powers of growth.
The land having been prepared by the plough
and harrow, in the manner before explained,
the seed is to be sown. There are three principal methods of performing this operation:—
namely, by *broadcast*, by *dibbing*, or by the
drill. The first is no doubt the most ancient
way; and considerable skill is required from,
and practised by, the husbandman, in performing this part of his duty. His walk, his throw,
his grasp, must each be accurately timed and
measured, or his ground and seed would be
greatly wasted, by having some spaces scarcely
supplied, and others so overdone, that the plant
would fail for want of room. He steps along
the furrows with great regularity, and flings at
such intervals, and in such quantities, as will
ensure the designed allowance, which varies a
little according to circumstances,—about two

bushels to the acre is usual. It is afterwards
harrowed in, and sometimes even ploughed;
and in a few days or weeks the tiny tender
blade appears, which has to endure the utmost
rigour of our winter season.

Nothing but experience could persuade us
that this is the best way to ensure the ensuing
harvest. Wheat of a certain sort is, indeed,
sown in the spring; but this is apt to produce
straw, rather than corn. The previous growth
of the root is needful, to sustain the productive
ears. The slender and blackened appearance
of the blade in winter does not much discou-
rage the farmer. The spring will impart strength
and freshness to the blade, unless the roots, by
being thrown from the earth by the frost, should
become, as the farmers term it, "winter killed."
To prevent this, a heavy roll should be applied
in the spring, which serves to settle the roots,

and enables them to obtain sufficient and timely aliment.

Wheat that is *dibbed,* or *dibbled,* is dropped, two or three kernels at a time, into holes, made by a man with a pointed instrument in the shape of a T. This he holds by the cross piece, and thrusts the longer leg, which is pointed with iron, into the ground, at the distance of a few inches, with considerable quickness as he walks. Children usually follow, and drop the seed into the holes which he makes. This mode of sowing wheat is unknown in the United States, but is not uncommon in England.

The *drill* is too complex a machine to be accurately described, or understood here. It is a sort of box, containing the wheat, borne on two wheels, and drawn by horses. The wheels, as they go round, give motion to a sort of cylinder within the box, in which are fixed instruments, like tea-spoons, at proper distances. Underneath are cutting irons, which form grooves, or drills, to receive the seed, as it is delivered from the spoons; and the process is thus completed with mechanical precision, such as pleases the eye, when the plant issues from the soil. However, the advantages of this contrivance, on the whole, are not so great, but that most of the English farmers proceed by the old method still. We must now leave the wheatfield for a season.

BARLEY is a grain and ear more nearly resembling wheat than any other grain. The character by which any may distinguish it, is the brush, or beard, consisting of long slender spikes, or needles, which proceed from each kernel, and extend considerably beyond the ear. The principal use of barley is for making

WINTER BARLEY.   SPRING BARLEY.

beer; in order for which, it first undergoes a process, called *malting*. It is also ground for bread in some countries; and is used also as food for hogs. It has, besides, many medicinal virtues. This grain is always sown in the spring of the year, in dry weather. Some of the early sorts are ready in nine or ten weeks. It is sometimes sown at two operations, and afterwards rolled, to press the earth close, and level it for the mower. It should be rolled when it has been up two or three weeks, which causes the plant to produce a greater number of stems.

OATS.—This is a beautiful variety of the corn tribe. The grain remains not in its case or ear, as in the former sorts, but, starting thence, hangs in single kernels, depending from the stalk, having a very light and graceful appearance. The minute seeds of various grasses

are thus arranged, and form some of the most
elegant of vegetable structures. The principal

OATS.

variety of oats cultivated in the United States
is the white kind. In England they have in

G

addition a black kind. White oats are most common near London, and black oats in the north. Dr. Johnson, who bore no kindly feeling towards Scotchmen and their country, said, in the first editions of his Dictionary, that oats were "food for horses in England, and men in Scotland."

I have said that wheat will *grow* almost any where; but there are many places where it does not *thrive*, and yet oats will do very well. In poor lands and wet seasons, these take less harm than other corn; and good oats may make even better bread than bad wheat. They are sown here sometimes in March, but generally not till April.

RYE is an inferiour grain, the ear of which somewhat resembles that of barley. It is,

however, much used for bread, especially in
the New-England states. In England, it is
sown chiefly as pasture food for cattle. Rye,

RYE.

of a bad quality, has, it is said, proved poison-
ous to its consumers, in some seasons.

PULSE, CROPS, &c.

THESE are so called, because they are supposed to be gathered by *pulling*, not by mowing or reaping; but, considered as farming produce, the meaning does not, in that respect, apply.

The chief pulse crops are peas and beans. These grow in pods.

Of PEAS we have many varieties, both early and late. They are extensively cultivated for the table, and are considered a rich and not unhealthful food. In the state of Vermont and in some of the western states, great quantities are raised as food for horses and swine. They also find their way into market, and are sold for soup and other table requisites. These last are generally called *field-peas*.

FIELD-PEA.

FIELD-BEANS in England, are chiefly raised for horses. In that country, the kind raised is smaller and darker coloured than the garden sorts. In the United States, especially in New-England, the white kind is most generally approved, and furnishes an excellent food for the table. Beans often yield a good crop, even on poor, sandy, or gravelly soil. With proper care this crop is as valuable as a wheat crop.

TARE.

In England they raise another sort of pulse called TARES, or Vetches, which are a *small*

sort of beans; grown not for the sake of the
seed, but for the green herb, as cattle food.
They are generally sowed early enough to
allow of being fed off, or cut, so as to make
room for a crop of turnips afterwards; or, if
the land is to be prepared for a wheat crop,
they are ploughed in as manure.

Cow Cabbages, called also *drum-heads*, are
grown on some farms in England to a considerable extent, and to a very large size. We
know little about them in this country for cattle.
The original stock, from which the cultivated
cabbage is derived, and from which also
colewort, borecole, cauliflowers, and brocoli,
have been obtained, grows on cliffs by the sea-
side, in the counties of Kent, Cornwall, York-
shire, and in Wales. In the wild state, we
should scarcely know this plant as a cabbage;

the leaves being few and extended, and destitute of the *heart* which is obtained by culture.

MUSTARD.

MUSTARD. —Of this plant there are two species, the black and the white; both natives of Great Britain. The white mustard is seldom cultivated in the United States, but is common in parts of England, where the plant is used as a salad. The seed is much used in its whole or unbroken state, as a medicine. In Spain, and some other countries of Europe, it is ground and used on the table, and is preferred, on account of its giving a whiter and milder flour, to the seed of the black.

Black mustard is chiefly cultivated in fields for the mill, and for medicinal purposes. It is extensively raised both in the United States and in England, but chiefly in small patches. It is sowed either in drills or broad-cast. The time of sowing is March or April, and the crop is gathered in July or August.

Vegetables in less demand than those I have named, or which are grown for the purposes of medicine or manufactures, do not form usual crops on farms in general; such as saffron,

madder, coriander, caraway, and some others.
Besides these, there are plants of vast importance for their respective uses, which are not to
be met with like corn and hay; as hops, hemp,
flax, and teasels. I shall notice these in their place.

SAFFRON.

SAFFRON is a kind of crocus: a preparation
of which is used in medicine, and in the art of

dyeing. In Cambridgeshire, in England, near the borders of Essex, this plant has long been cultivated to a great extent. Saffron Walden derives its name from this product of its vicinity. As soon as the flowers of this plant appear, they are gathered by hand, in the morning, before they open; a part of the flower is afterwards picked out; this being subjected to heat and pressure, forms a cake, which is the drug that bears the name. Saffron in small quantities is raised by almost every family in New-England, and is used in its unprepared state in various complaints. It is only for the sake of convenience that it is formed into a cake.

MADDER is produced in many parts of England and Holland, and in small quantities in the United States; and the roots of it, when peeled, dried, and powdered, supply a beautiful red colour, without which, those whose business it is to dye cloths, would, to a great extent, be

MADDER.

inconvenienced. So insinuating is the colouring property of this plant, that animals who feed upon it have their very bones stained of a ruddy hue. Madder is also employed in medicine. An acre will produce about two thousand pounds of dry, saleable madder. It usually sells for about thirty-two dollars per hundred.

CORIANDER.

CORIANDER is frequently sown with teasel and caraway, in England, because these last do not come to perfection until the second year; so that the coriander may be harvested without injury to them. It is cultivated solely for the sake of the small globular seeds, which are used by distillers, druggists, and confectioners, to impart an aromatic or pungent flavour. It is sometimes mixed with dough to flavour bread. It is raised only in small quantities in the United States, and chiefly in gardens.

CARAWAY SEEDS, I need not say, are employed in the same way; although, as substitutes for plums or currants, I always thought them, when a boy, quite an imposition of the cook. The plant grows wild in many places in England, of which country it is a native. It is harvested in July, and threshed out in the field. We raise it only in our garden, or in small patches in the field.

HOPS.

HOPS.

THE hop plant is a native of Britain, in parts of which it is raised on a large scale, especially in the county of Kent. It is also raised to a considerable extent in parts of the United States. The English seem not to have been aware of its use, until they learned it from the Continent, in the reign of Henry VIII. Without the dried flower-buds of this plant, which are the hops of commerce, barley-wine, or ale, would be unpalatable, and a quickly-spoiling drink ; so that, unless some substitute for hops were used of old, the "nut-brown-ale," of which the ancient English ballads tell, could scarcely have been entitled to the praise which it has received.

I suppose I scarcely need say, that this is a winding, climbing plant, arising from a root that continues many years in the ground, although the plant itself perishes at the close of every season. A hop-plantation requires several summers' growth, before it is in good order for produce. The plants begin to appear about the month of April or May. When they are a few inches above ground, poles, about twenty feet high, are driven in for them to twist themselves upon. The season for the hop-harvest in England is about the middle of September, but somewhat later with us; and a busy, busfling time it is in the great hop countries. Men, women, and children, now find plenty to do for some weeks. The method is this: long and large boxes, or baskets, are prepared. The plants are cut off close to the earth, and the poles being pulled out, are laid across those baskets with the binds upon them; the hops are then picked off.

The next process is collecting and drying them in a kiln; after which they are housed for some days in the stowage rooms; and, at

H

last, forced into bags by the foot and leaden weights.   The persons who perform this are called *packers*.

The best hops are put into finer bags, which are called *pockets*; the inferiour sort only are called *bags*. When the picking is accomplished, the binds, or stalks, are cleared from the poles, which are stacked or piled together, for future occasions. The haulm, or straw of the plant, is used by the poorer classes in England for fuel, and is sometimes burnt on the soil for manure.

Hops are a very uncertain crop; and therefore a most anxious speculation to growers, in England, whose chief support is derived from this branch of business.

A heavy duty is laid upon them in England; consequently, the excise officers watch the whole process, lest frauds on the revenue should be committed. Of the woody part of the stalk, after it has been soaked in water, a coarse kind of paper may be made.

This brings us to notice plants, which are especially cultivated as materials for manufacture. I mean HEMP, FLAX, and TEASELS.

HEMP, FLAX, AND TEASELS.

HEMP.

HEMP is one of the herbaceous plants, and grows to the height of five or six feet. It has a stiffish stalk, narrow finger-formed leaves,

and inconsiderable flowers. It might easily be
passed by, as a weed of worthless form, by un-
informed persons. There is, however, scarcely
a plant that grows, excepting those essential for
food, which ranks with this in importance. It
forms the ropes and cables which belong to the
ship; and its use in the unnumbered forms of
thread, twine, ropes, canvas, sacking, and other
cloths, is beyond estimation.

The principal country for hemp, as an article
of commerce, is Russia; few other countries
grow even enough for their own consumption.
It is, indeed, cultivated in some parts of Britain;
particularly in Suffolk and Norfolk, and within
a few years has been introduced into the United
States. The soil which suits it best, is a moist,
loose, sandy loam. It is sown in April or May,
and the plants are ready for pulling up in three

or four months. That which is ready first, is called *fimble;* the latter, *karle,* or *seed hemp.*

As soon as the plant is pulled, it is tied in bundles, and set up to dry ; at the end of about ten days, the bundles are loosened at the top, and the heads are held upon a hurdle by one person, whilst another threshes out the seed with a small flail.

The hemp is prepared for manufacture by being spread out on the field to dry, so that the weather may separate the fibres; or else it is steeped some days in stagnant water. The next thing is to cleanse away the bark from the stalks. This is either done by the hand, or by machinery constructed for the purpose. It is afterwards beaten in mills, and then combed, or dressed, by drawing it through instruments called *hackles,* like those used by wool-combers and others.

The commodity is then easily enough spun into thread, twisted into ropes, or woven into cloth, according to the required purpose.

Hemp-seeds are used as food for poultry; and an oil, of some value, is obtained from them. The inner woody stalks (for it is the bark only which is manufactured) are used in countries, where fuel is scarce, by the poorer classes, instead of wood.

FLAX is another herbaceous plant, but of a much finer fibre and quality than hemp, and capable also of being bleached to snowy whiteness. Need I say that *linen* is hence obtained?

It is supposed that this incalculably useful plant originally came from Egypt. Cotton, it is true, now supplies largely its place, and is every year making the demand for flax still less.

This plant is cultivated with considerable success in many parts of England and the United States. Like hemp, it is sown in the

FLAX.

spring; and the plants, when ready, are pulled up by the roots. Both stem and seed are objects of importance. The latter, commonly called *linseed*, yields a valuable drying oil for the painter's use, and for other purposes. A liquor is also obtained from this seed, by means of boiling water, which our nurses call *linseed tea*, and which is accounted useful for coughs, and other diseases proceeding from irritation of the throat and lungs.

The flax intended for linen is conveyed in bundles to the place where it is to undergo the process of watering; there it is thrown into ponds of soft stagnant water, in which it is kept for several days. By this means the bark is detached. The bundles are then laid out on the grass, in regular rows, till the flax separates from the stalks on being rubbed between the hands. After various dressings, similar to those of hemp, it is fit for the manufacturer's use.

Now for TEASELS.—These are plants some-what resembling thistles. When the flower has faded, the seeds are contained in a sort of

TEASELS.

honey-comb structure, shaped like an egg, abounding in small hooks, of a hard and stub-born substance. This teasel head, with its scratching hooks, is used by the wool-combers for raising what is called *the nap* on cloths. Several of the heads are fixed, either on boards or to the outer circle of a large wheel, by which the purpose is accomplished. Nature supplies us with abundance of *materials*, but with very few *tools*, like the teasel head, ready for our use!

Fields of teasels, which are to be seen in some places, are not the most convenient thoroughfares for persons in flowing robes, very few of which would be left on the backs of such as might be compelled to hurry through them.

I rather think that, farmer as I call myself, I have omitted to take any account of a very material article of agricultural produce, which should have been noticed whilst treating of corn.

Well then, I suppose I must say that the stalks of grain, and some other plants, are called STRAW; and as this article covers houses, litters horses, manures the land, forms the door-mat to the cottage and the head-covering of the ladies, a word or two must be spared about it; more especially, as I have not forgotten such things as caraway seeds and teasels.

Wheat straw, in England, being the strongest and longest, is so much better than any other, that little else is sent to market for common use. In the United States we prefer *Rye straw*, which is generally longer, brighter, and pos-sesses greater strength.

After threshing, it is either stacked by itself, or gathered and tied in what we term *bundles*,

but which by the English are called *trusses*.
Thirty-six trusses, each weighing thirty-six
pounds, in that country, form a load of straw.
We generally sell it by the ton. This commodity is disposed of in the markets in the same
manner as hay.

I may just add here, that the stalks of potatoes, beans, and some other such plants, have,
in England, the appropriate name of *haulm*. I
wish this term was common with us.

———————

It is evident that, owing to the varied qualities
of land, and the equally varying management
which the numerous vegetable productions
require, a farmer, if ignorant, unskilful, or
negligent, will soon find an enemy in every
circumstance around him. The wrong time,

or the wrong place, or the wrong method, will make his labour the most costly folly to which, probably, he could addict himself. Not many, however, of those who have been brought up to the business, err to this extent: it is *chiefly* those who turn from other pursuits to this, who find out, when too late, that they have not knowledge and industry enough, even to become a farmer!

LIVE STOCK.

OXEN.

THIS part of the produce of the farm, is that by which the occupier realizes, frequently, the principal part of his profits. Americans are fond of good living; and would consider they dined poorly indeed, if they had no other viands than the choicest vegetable productions. They must enjoy the substantial and savoury blessings of beef and bacon, mutton, lamb, and veal, and all the varieties of poultry and of game, or they (at least the wealthier classes) think themselves objects of compassion, restricted to *vegetable diet!*

Well then, as they are able and willing to pay for these things, we farmers and graziers endeavour to supply their wants; and are not sorry to have another way of disposing of our vegetable produce, besides the sale of it for money. By feeding animals which are required for the table, we get rid of our grass, hay, corn, and other things, in a more advantageous manner, than if we were obliged to sell all for others to consume.

The first on the list of meats, undoubtedly, must be beef.

The Ox—in a wild state called the *Bison*—is an animal comprising the most useful assemblage of qualities and materials for the varied necessities of man in a civilized condition, of any creature with which nature has supplied him. Cattle of this class yield subsistence, living or dead; and this in greater abundance, of course, than the other sorts, which are inferiour in size. A Cow may be compared to a sum of money, from which a man may take continually without diminishing his store; for the *carcass* we may call the *principal*, and the milk and calves the *interest*. There is, indeed, this difference in favour of the animal as property, that she will yield in a year, perhaps, twice the value of her purchase and food; whilst the same sum in money will not generally yield in the public funds much more than a twentieth part of its own amount as interest.

In enumerating the uses to which the body of this creature is applicable, we must reckon up all the different substances of which it is composed: the flesh, the fat, the intestines, the blood, the bones, the skin, the hair, the hoofs, the horns. For the use of the *flesh*, or *beef*, I will merely request my young friends to ask themselves the question at their usual dinner hour. That portion of the *fat* which is not eaten with the flesh, helps to form candles and soap. The *blood* is employed largely in the purification of sugar, and in some other manufacturing processes. Of the *bones* are made knife and fork handles. The *skin* interposes, in the form of leather, between the tender foot of man and the harsh or humid soil. The *hair* serves, in the mixture of mortar, for plasterers, to give it a tenacity, or power of holding together, which is most important for walls so covered; the *hoofs* and *horns*, dissolved by heat, are moulded into almost any form for various implements of incessant utility —such as handles, combs, and lanthorn panes. The clippings, parings, and refuse of the hide, and other parts, are boiled down to a jelly, which, being strained, purified, and pressed into moulds, constitutes *glue*, without which our chairs and tables would fall in pieces.

With regard to the purchase, sale, and management by the farmer, of these and other animals, of which I shall have to speak, little need be said in this place. They have their varieties, in kind and quality: they have, too, their diseases; and there are different modes of treating them, according to varying customs, circumstances, and climates. These cattle are less dainty, as feeders in a pasture, than the horse and the sheep; and leave fewer *orts*, or refuse food, behind them. In winter, they need hay and turnips. The latter, sometimes, are lodged even in their capacious throats; when an instrument, called a choaking rope—a remedy which to us would be worse than the disease—is used to push it down. A worse misfortune, at times, is occasioned by the animals feeding too freely on growing clover, which distends them to bursting and death, unless an incision be seasonably performed.

SHEEP.

The sheep comes second in the rank of animals destined for the service of our race. The Creator, with a power and wisdom infinitely great, *varies* the qualities of His unnumbered gifts. A sheep differs altogether from an ox; even more in nature than in size. Mutton, as food, is a change, which the health, perhaps, as well as the appetite, approves, and constitutes a large portion of the meat with which our tables are supplied.

But the sheep does more for us in the way of clothing than in food, by resigning to us, yearly, its ample coat. Wool has a property different entirely from that of other hair; for its constant tendency to curl and wrinkle, causes it, when woven, to thicken up, and make a closer texture, as it is manufactured. This surprisingly important quality renders woollen garments the chief clothing of civilized man; and, in consequence, the wool is the means of subsistence to thousands of manufacturers in different countries of the world.

Sheep-shearing in the United States is only performed once in the year. In warmer climates, application is twice made in the season to this compliant animal for his suit of clothes. We generally have ours sheared in the latter part of May, or early in June, when the state of the weather renders the operation at least safe to the sheep. The performance is rather a rough and toilsome one to, I believe, all concerned. The animals have first to be washed, which is repugnant enough, I doubt not, to the subjects of it, who are generally averse to water. The shearing is any thing but play to the shearer and the shorn. Great strength and dexterity are required in the man; and nothing less than the proverbial patience of the sheep to render the operation possible. The wool is cut exceedingly close; and there seems, indeed, great danger, as the instrument snaps along, that flesh, as well as the coat, will go. But they are rarely injured, unless succeeding chilly weather renders the loss of wool an uncomfortable privation.

Sheep and lambs are liable to various accidents and diseases.

The LAMBS, coming at a time when the season is frequently severe, are very likely to perish, without great care. Both sheep and lambs, being utterly defenceless animals, are also commonly the property most likely to suffer from thieves and dogs, notwithstanding the utmost caution of their owner.

The fat of sheep congeals more readily than that of oxen, and is much used for tallow. The skins, when dressed, form that useful substance called *wash-leather*. The intestines form the article erroneously called *catgut,* used for musical and mechanical purposes. The varieties of this animal are also many.

HOGS.

Here is an animal, differing from the other sorts exactly in those particulars which render it capable of occupying a place in the service of man, which, otherwise, must remain vacant and unproductive; with many of the poor it is invaluable, as being the only animal of the numerous farming herds that can subsist on the

common and scanty means which are open to
them. The cow and the sheep must have pasture, and often costly care. Not so the poor
man's pig: with an unfailing appetite, he pos-
sesses incessant industry, and an universal
taste, or relish, for almost any substances,
animal or vegetable, of the select, or refuse
kind, which come under the cognizance of his
oblique, judicious eye, and his accurate and
laborious nose.

If swine be a treasure to the cottager, they
can scarcely be less so to the farmer, whose
yard and stubble-fields are strewed with scattered food, which, but for the hogs, would be
entirely lost. But these creatures, naturally
roaming, though herding together, do not con-
fine themselves to their owner's domain. In
the autumn they sometimes absent themselves
for weeks in the woods and thickets, in search

of their natural food, the fruits of the oak, the hazel, and the beech, and those earth-nuts and esculent roots, which their acute sense of smell, and ploughing snout enable them to find.

As the flesh of pigs is in high request, when young, for the table, and, when large, forms a staple commodity, cured and dried as bacon, we farmers, besides consuming a great deal ourselves, find an important advantage in this sort of stock; and he is a bad manager, or very poor indeed, who does not, at the proper season, take care to be supplied with a sufficient store.

HORSES.

I have placed first such animals as are used for food, because it is the kind of produce, of the live sort, to which the farmer chiefly looks for a return in money. If, however, animals are

8 . K

to be ranked according to their apparent station in sagacity, dignity, and beauty, the horse should certainly be the first on the list. But I am only treating of animals as they concern the farm; and, therefore, do not profess to class or describe them as the naturalist would do.

In Great Britain, farmers make great use of the horse in the cultivation of their lands. In this country, we prefer oxen. In light soils, horses answer a good purpose. They are quicker than oxen, and hence the farmer can perform with them more ploughing in a day than with oxen. Yet in this country we think the advantage lies on the side of oxen, as they are more hardy, and when no longer fit for the yoke, may be fatted, and thus yield the farmer a profit, which cannot be said of the superannuated horse.

Farming horses should be of the larger sort.

Their labour on the road, as well as in the field, is heavy. Loads of hay, corn, manure, &c., generally try their strength much, and require a good team.

There is much in the care and management of horses, whether at work or in the stable, which makes the difference in their usefulness and condition. Plenty of food is one thing, but by no means the only point of importance. With regard to their work, judgment and gentleness in those who guide them will get more service out of this sensitive animal, than all the blows and ill usage which can be resorted to. The carman, wagoner, ploughman, horseman, or whoever he may be that attends them, should, to be master of his business, understand the mechanical means, as to the harness and machine, by which his horses' strength is applied. He should understand the language which the animal also understands; and find out the temper of the different animals, which varies much, and cultivate a good understanding with each of his speechless but sensible companions in toil. It is well known, that where one man can do nothing with a horse, another can, with ease, induce him to perform wonders. The management of these and other animals, is, indeed, quite a talent, and a very valuable one, in a farming man.

The carter or wagoner always walks (ride he ought not) on the left, or *near* side of the horse, or vehicle; because, as the rule is to let things pass him on the right, or *off* side, he would otherwise be placed between the two carriages, to his great inconvenience or danger. "Gee!" is the word, which makes the horse turn to the right; and "Come hither, woa!" the injunction which draws him towards the left;

accompanied, sometimes, by passing the whip lightly over the neck.

When hay, or any other heavy load is placed in a cart, to which a horse is attached, care and judgment are necessary to adjust the weight with respect to a balance, so that it may neither *bear* nor hang too much; for, if placed too much in front, the stoutest horse might have his back broken by the pressure. On the contrary, if it is placed too much behind, it may even force him up from the ground.

The food of horses used for labour is grass, hay, oats, chaff, peas, beans, bran, and sometimes roots, as carrots, and even parsnips. A change and mixture of food is generally beneficial. Wheat, given in any considerable quantity, will kill a horse.

The careful and successful farmer is never contented to let the management of his horses go entirely from under his own eye. He enters the stable, and sees that they are not only fed and watered, but well groomed, well littered, and made comfortable and safe for the night; and this he does, even though he may have reason to think his men are themselves proud of their team. A few days since I found my thoughtless boy putting one of my best horses, "Blackbird," into the cart, to go to the mill, although he had cast a shoe. But perhaps I ought not to expect him to mind his business, if I, by sitting here scribbling, neglect my own.

THE DAIRY AND POULTRY-YARD.

HAVING concluded all that I think useful to say about farming horses, I will next say a word or two respecting the dairy and poultry.

I have living in my family a clever old domestic, by the name of Susan, who has long superintended the dairy, and has made, perhaps, as much butter as would freight a ship; and churned as much milk as would float it! Her powers are not now equal to her will and her skill; a fact, however, of which she is not aware, and which it would offend her grievously to mention. So we make the best of it; and render her what assistance she needs, without hinting at all, that she cannot do as she

DAIRY.

could fifty years ago, when, a ruddy lass of twenty, she was first hired by my grandmother, in the kitchen.

I believe, if I could make Susan understand that I was pretending to print in a book any part of the business of the dairy, or hen-houses, she would think the subject as much beyond my knowledge, as I consider natural philosophy to be above hers. As I am quite certain she will never read my writings, I will venture to proceed with the best information I possess.

I suppose I need not say that the material, the management of which, makes the business of the dairy, is *milk*. This kindly and healthful fluid, the benign sustenance of the infant from its birth, and, in one form or another, of man in all periods of his life, is produced by various animals in quantity sufficient to afford

L

to their possessors an important measure of their food. That of cows is chiefly used in the United States, as being more palatable, and better adapted for those changes into solid forms, which we require in butter and in cheese. It is the process of transformation into those substances of which I am now to speak.

The oily and thicker parts of milk naturally separate, on being left undisturbed for some time. The *cream*, as we then call it, forms a yellow coat at the top, which is easily skimmed off and placed in separate vessels; but this, without further operations, would never become either butter or cheese. To make butter, a violent mechanical agitation is necessary; to accomplish which, various simple machines, called *churns*, have been invented. I believe the oldest sort used both in England and the United States, is the common upright churn, consisting of a high, narrow tub, with a stick, or stirrer, passing through the lid. To the lower end of this stick is fastened a flat round board, not quite so wide as the diameter of the churn: this is the *beater;* and being moved rapidly up and down, will in time make good butter.

But the best and most expeditious churn is, perhaps, in the form of a barrel, supported on a frame, and whirled round and round by a winch. The time required for the continuance of this motion, before *the butter comes,* as they say, varies much, according to the nature of the milk, and the management of it, from one hour, to half a day. When sufficiently formed, the butter is taken out, and pressed with great care, to rid it of the remaining fluid, called *butter-milk,* which would soon turn it sour Such as is intended for present use, or sale, is called *fresh butter.* It is put up in different

ways in different countries. In some it is formed into moulds, measures, or lengths. In and
near London, it is sold in lumps, by the pound;
in other parts, in portions named from fluid
measures, as pints and quarts of butter. Go a
little farther, and you must ask for *half a yard,
or a yard,* of butter, according to your need.

Salt butter is packed in firkins, and pickled,
or salted, to preserve it for a length of time.
Many tricks are played by dishonest persons in
this business to increase the apparent weight,
or bulk, and to impose a bad article for a good
one. Sometimes it is packed hollow, with
water between; or bad butter is placed within,
and good, just at the ends of the firkin. So
much has been done in this way, that an act of
parliament, in England, has been made ex-
pressly against it.

In England, Epping and Dorset butter have

each a name in the market; and vast quantities are sold as such, which could never possibly have been produced at those places. This commodity is a most important article of commerce; fifty thousand tons weight being annually consumed in London only.

Cheese is another form, in .which milk becomes manufactured into a substantial article of food, and, therefore, of trade. The mere process is simple and easy enough. The milk is curdled—that is, the more solid parts are separated from the whey, by a small quantity of a liquor, called *rennet*, prepared from the inner skin of a calf's stomach. The curds, after being cleared of the whey, are collected together, subjected to a strong pressure in moulds, or bags, and then dried for use. In the United States the cheese in greatest favour is Goshen cheese. The town of Goshen is situated in the northern part of the state of Connecticut. The people of Boston, however, and its vicinity, receive much of the cheese which is made in several parts of Massachusetts, particularly in New Braintree, in the county of Worcester. Large quantities of excellent cheese are annually brought to the Boston market, chiefly in consequence of a large premium which is annually offered by an association in that city for the best three lots of butter which may be presented. Excellent cheese is produced in various other parts of our country.

In England, much is thought of the Cheshire, Gloucestershire, and other kinds of cheese. That which gives the peculiar flavour to Cheshire, and other cheeses, is, I believe, chiefly, the quality of the pastures on which the cows feed. Besides this, I have understood that other materials, such as suet, and colouring matter, are commonly added.

That which is accounted the richest of all English cheese, is the *Stilton;* not made, however, at the place of that name, but in various parts of the midland counties. It is not reckoned in its prime till it is two years old, and decayed, blue, and moist. I will only add, before I pass to my next subject, that Parmesan cheese, made in Italy, is composed of a mixture of ewe's or goat's milk with that of the cow, and is much esteemed at the tables of the wealthy.

THE POULTRY-YARD.

The species of fowls which best reward man for his protection and supplies, are four: turkeys, geese, common fowls, as they are called, and ducks.

Turkeys are natives of America, and were formerly found in the forests in great abundance. They were first taken to England in the middle of the sixteenth century. They are by far the largest, and, as some think, the finest birds used for food in this or any other country. On account of the estimation in which they are held, and the price they consequently bear, they become objects of attention in many poultry-yards. At Christmas time, such supplies of these dainty birds are required for the city of London, that coaches, it is said, are often loaded with them, to the exclusion of other passengers.

Turkeys are the most tender and difficult to rear of all our fowls; so that the money they fetch is sometimes scarcely a compensation for the trouble and their food. They must be fed for some time after they are hatched, with a sort

of pudding, made with milk and eggs. The
hen-turkey is by no means so good a provider,
defender, and teacher of her young, as the
common hen. When, therefore, numbers are
to be reared, those duties must be chiefly performed by man. When of sufficient age, grain
and barley-meal will do for their food, without
which, although they pick about for insects, they
would not attain sufficient bulk or fatness for
the table.

Common fowls, though disposed of at a common price, are more profitable, in general, than
the rarer sorts, because they provide for themselves to a great extent. I think there are
nearly thirty hens in my yard, with I know not
how many broods of young chickens. Half as
many turkeys would require a yard full of people to take care of them; but these, though
they need daily feeding, procure by far the

9

greater part of their own subsistence by incessant assiduity. The hens are admirable and complete managers of their young, whom they provide for, teach, and defend, in the most competent manner imaginable. It is curious to observe the old hens, when they have discovered a particle of food, calling their brood around them, by a peculiar cluck, which the young ones well understand, breaking it for them with the bill, if too large, and standing by, perhaps hungry at the time, scarcely taking a grain for themselves. Then again as to fierceness and courage, deficient as the hen is in these qualities when herself only is in danger, she becomes a winged dragon for her young, not hesitating to attack, with successful fury, animals twenty times her superior in strength.

Hen-houses should have boxes partitioned for the nests, and poles for the fowls to roost on at night, provided with a sort of step-ladders by which the little ones may ascend, before they can use their wings. The hen sits on her eggs for about twenty-one days, with such determined perseverance, that she will almost perish on her nest, rather than remit her duty. Humanity requires that these poor animals should not thus be suffered to injure or destroy themselves by the vain continuance of their endeavours to warm into life eggs which cannot be hatched. Long after they quit the shell, the young chickens find warmth and shelter beneath the parent's wing; and will even run to it, sometimes, when far too large to be conveniently protected.

In about three months, the chickens are fit for the table, or for stores. They are commonly fattened, under coops, before they are killed; though, for my own part, I think a barn-door fowl, — that is, one which has had the full run of the yard, is quite as palatable, and perhaps more wholesome meat, than one gorged with excessive feeding, without exercise, or the enjoyment of its own notions of quantity and selection.

The *eggs* produced in the winter months, are by no means an unprofitable store at Christmas and the festive season. Five and six cents, in hard winters, have sometimes been given for an egg.

The poultry-yard is sometimes exposed to the depredations of quite a merciless foe — the fox. Formerly our farmers were greatly annoyed by these animals, and were obliged to secure their poultry-house, as they did their granaries. If, however, at any time, reynard obtained admittance, the defenceless birds were drawn, one after another, from the roost, and slain with as little humanity about it, as is felt by a native savage in the moment of his proudest victory. Whilst the fox attacks the birds, rats, skunks, weasels, and other vermin, make equal havoc with the eggs; sucking or carrying them away with astonishing secrecy and despatch.

Geese are not always inhabitants of the farmer's premises; for, as they feed with a somewhat unsavoury spoon on the meadow-grass, horses and other animals do not much relish their leavings;—in fact, they will not, if they can help it, feed after them. It is where there is an open green, or common, with ponds of water, that these birds thrive best, and do their owners most good. They are to a proverb stupid; yet have sense enough, in general, for their occasions. They know their home; and, at the close of evening, resort thither in a row, without confusion, or the least diversity of purpose.

These animals will live almost entirely on grass; and cost, therefore, very little, where they can do no harm. About Christmas they are in season, and in the greatest request; and the number disposed of in the markets then is very great.

There are two orders of beings to whom the public are especially indebted for their literary treasures—I mean geese and authors. It is lucky when the quill does not come a second time into the possession of a goose, or one of similar capacity. The demand for quills is so great, that vast flocks of geese are kept in the fens of Lincolnshire, in England, and elsewhere, to produce the required supply. Unfortunately for the poor birds, their feathers are in great request too, for bedding; so that they are plucked alive, five times in the year, for feathers, and their wings once, for their unrivalled quills.

In respect to *ducks*, as they do not graze, or scratch the soil, farmers need not be afraid of any mischief from them, and they require small attention and supplies. They do not hatch so early as hens; and, therefore, it is common to put some of their eggs under a sitting hen, who will perform the office as well as if they were her own. She is, however, sadly perplexed and frightened, when her brood, notwithstanding all her care and clucking, take to the water, according to their nature.

I have now, I believe, mentioned the principal animals which the farmer maintains for his use or profit in this country. There are others, which, unfortunately, he is compelled to keep, to his own great inconvenience and damage;—these are the species of depredators, of which I have elsewhere spoken as vermin.

In England, the farmers experience one inconvenience, from which, in this republican country, we are exempted. There, laws are in force, the design of which is to prevent the common people from killing most wild animals, and birds, fit for eating. These are preserved for the benefit and pleasure of the higher orders. And, indeed, as they form the great inducement to the gentry to reside during a part of the year on their estates, and so spend some of their money in the country, it would certainly be unwise to destroy or extirpate entirely, even if the laws permitted people so to do. The farmer, however, often suffers severely from the appetites of these creatures, at the same time that he is forbidden to indulge his own with one of their number in return.

M

HAY-MAKING

THE season of hay making is generally one of the most delightful in the whole year. It usually begins in this country about the 20th of June. If the weather be fine, all is now bustle and activity throughout the country. The farmers in general are in fine health; although they may get but little sleep, they work day after day with great animation.

It is usual, during this season, for men who are professed mowers to go round the country to supply the extra demand for hands, during the gathering in of the hay-harvest. They find their own tools, and make the best bargain they can with their employers, working either by time or by the piece, as may be agreed on.

From five to six shillings an acre is, I believe, a very common price for mowing. Often the price is still more, if the grass be very stout, or the land uneven.

The apparently simple and easy operation of cutting the tender blades and stems of grass with the scythe, is admitted by master and man to be the most severe bodily exertion among all rural employments. The strain upon the back and arms is very great; and many strong men are wearied out by it, especially at first. There is also an important measure of knack and skill required for whetting, setting, and holding the blade, or the labor is intolerably increased, and the consequence would be a scored and ill-cut field.

To be better understood, I will proceed to a small enclosure, in which are six men, set on to mow.

Pray how do my little city friends suppose these six men proceed with their six scythes mowing down this piece of grass? "How! why they need not consider long about that," perhaps you reply; "each may begin in any part, and leave off when all is mown." Not so, if you please:—they might, if they had no plan of operation, miss portions, or meet casually, or follow carelessly, and cut each other's feet. The way is this: one commences alone at the side of the field, and cuts a few *swaths*; that is, by the sweep of his scythe he clears a certain space, and leaves the grass he has cut, in a straight row on his left hand as he goes on. This first man in time and place is called "my lord." When he has got a few paces forward, the second man begins also at the side of the piece, and just where the sweep of his own scythe will take off a similar width, without leaving any standing between his pathway and that of him who precedes him. This second man also leaves the swath in a line at his left hand, which forms another row. In the same way, when he has got far enough away, the third man begins, and so on, if there were twenty. It is easy to see that in this way no man can interfere with his companion's work. All is regular, and there is no danger of patches being left undone, to require a second visit. When the field is thus cut, the grass is said to be "*lying in the swaths.*" In this state it is best to lie, if rains should come on, or appear probable. At any rate, it is not usual to disturb it, until the mowers are out of the field; unless, on the other hand, it should happen to be propitiously fine after much showery weather.

Shaking-out is generally performed in the United States by boys; but in England by the women and children of the village. For this operation any one can see that the regular method in which the grass has been laid by the mowers, makes the employment regular and easy. The same plan is adopted. One takes the first row, and the second follows on the next, and so on. Now, we would not thank any one to work, even for nothing, who should conclude that the grass may be tossed about with the fork, as a cow might do it with her horns. If we have not sufficient confidence in the day to shake it fairly out, we order the swaths, which, perhaps, have lain already a day, to be just *turned over*, without much disturbing the mass as it grew together. If otherwise, the separation of the swath must be complete. We do not allow *lumps* of grass to be thrown about, portions of ground to remain uncovered, and so on; but the entangled knots must be fairly parted on the fork, the grass must be evenly spread, and the party are to work in neighbouring rows until the whole be completed.

I must not be too long in the hay-field; and therefore proceed more briefly in my account of the business. The next thing to be done, after the grass has had the best part of the day's sun, is to put it again into forms, called *wind-rows*. Wooden rakes, or the hay-forks, are used for this purpose. It is then not so much exposed to the dews of the night; and by lying in a sort of ridge, light and hollow, admits of the wind passing through it, which has nearly a similar effect with the sun, in drying the herb.

A little knowledge and experience are re-quired to enable persons to judge when the grass has lain long enough, and had a sufficient exposure to the sun and air. In very hot burning weather, one day will make it into hay; but this seldom happens. Generally the wind-rows have to be raked into small heaps, called cocks, several times, if not against rain, at least as a protection from the dews of the night. Hay-makers never commence this part of their work, until about eight o'clock in the morning, in order to allow previous time for the dews to evaporate. Should the weather continue good, in three or four days the hay is made and ready for carting. Carts, with large ladders before and behind, or wagons, are drawn into the field. Strong men are now employed to pitch and load: that is, to thrust up bundles of the hay on long-handled forks, whilst others in the vehicle receive it at their hands, and dispose it so as to ride well in a large mass. So much, indeed, will they cram in, and lay on, that the load seems as large as a considerable stack, almost concealing the oxen, whilst it moves slowly along the mead.

Stacking the hay, is another operation which requires knowledge and practice. A spot is generally selected for this purpose, which lies high and dry. A foundation is first laid of bushes, faggots, or logs, formed into a square of about the size required for the supposed quantity. When the load comes up, one man stands to receive and deposit the hay on this foundation, whilst another delivers it from the cart. If care be not taken in stacking, the hay will be laid in curly bundles and irregular knots, which will not cut and bind well; but we seldom have faults of that sort to complain of. The great danger is, in stacking the hay too green, or a little damp; in which case, if the rick be large, as fifty or sixty loads, the chance

10   N

STACKING HAY.

of its taking fire, or consuming without flame inwardly, is very great.

I never remember such a burst of rustic mirth as occurred one day—I think it was in the first summer I spent on a farm—when I said the hay was so dry, I was afraid it would take fire! I had heard of hay-stacks burning of themselves, and could not conceive that it could be when they were at all wet. My ignorance was made more amusing to them, and painful to me, by a good deal of conceited positiveness on my part, which would not for a long time give way to the repeated assurances of others, who had had fifty years' experience. Those husbandmen could not, of course, explain to me, that a chemical action, called *fermentation*, takes place, when herbage is laid together in a mass, and that this effect is generally more or less, in proportion to the degree

of moisture present in the heap. This fermentation creates a sort of inflammable gas, or
air, which, if produced in too great quantities,
exceeds the due degree of heat, and at length
consumes the fermenting body. The process
of fermentation, to a certain extent, is required
to make good hay in the stack—or, as they
say, it must have *a heat*. As it warms, it settles and subsides so much, that the rick appears, in a few days, scarcely half the height
which it was when first set up. Sometimes it
settles on one side; and occasionally, if managed by unskilful hands, it will topple fairly
over, and require complete rebuilding. This is
a vexatious occurrence to those concerned,
when, perhaps, great exertions are requisite to
do the work of this busy season once.

Whilst we are about the stack, I would describe to my readers the manner in which

stacks are thatched in England. It is a great preventive against rot and mould. The heating and settling having taken place, so as to render it safe to house in the stack, persons, whose business it is, are employed for this purpose. The roof being formed, or topped-up to a sufficient height, with any inferiour sort of hay, the thatcher and his *yelmer* go to work. Having prepared pegs and rods of split hazel, for pinning and binding down their work, the yĕlmer gets his straw in a heap, and splashes it pretty liberally with water. He then forms it into small lengthy bundles with his hands, and with such art, that these bundles shall frequently be longer than the straws of which they are composed, by being drawn out at each end. The thatcher then mounts his ladder; and, being supplied with these bundles, or *yelms*, as fast as he needs them, he bends each double near the end, and twists it into a sort of knot; then, beginning at the eaves, he tucks this part of the bundle so far into the hay, as to detain it there, the ends of the straw hanging out. Having placed an even row of these, he inserts another row just over them, the ends of each new row lying half over the row which went before. Thus the straws lie one over another, like the hairs on a cat's back, up to the very ridge, which is, afterwards, either bound down close, or made with a stiff edging of straw in an upright position. The whole is firmly secured by long, bent, and notched pegs, driven far into the stack. The edges and eaves are afterwards clipped straight with proper shears.

When the stack has been well set up, the sides properly pulled, (that is, the outside looser hay drawn out, so as to shew a flat, firm surface,) when the thatching has been accomplished by a clever hand, and all litters cleared away, the hay-rick is no mean specimen of mechanical skill, or practical cleverness. This will stand uninjured, and do the farmer credit and service, after two or three seasons have passed over; whereas, when slovenly careless hands have done every thing wrong, instead of right, the heap looks like a dung-hill, and probably becomes one, from the rain soaking through the ill-managed, half-finished roof.

HAY-BINDING AND SELLING.

Poor farmers, who want money before it is advantageously to be had, seldom let their produce remain long in the rick-yard, or barn. They often send it to market, and lose by it, because they cannot wait a few months for better terms.

Farms near Boston or New-York have the readiest opportunities for this sort of proceeding. The markets there ensure a certain sale for agricultural goods, provided the sellers will consent to the *selling* price, which, when the market is full, is often very low.

Hay is a commodity equally familiar to our city and country readers, loaded in carts or wagons for the buyer.

The process of getting it to market in this country is quite simple. Hay, which is sold, is usually sheltered in a barn, and when about to be taken to market, it is put on to a cart or wagon and weighed. It is sold by the ton.

In England, much of the hay which is carried to market is taken from the stacks. Let us see how the farmers there manage.

A part of the thatch having been removed from one corner, the cutter pulls out a quantity of the inferiour hay, which formed the stack towards the roof; and, taking it down in a bundle, sprinkles it with water until it is very wet. His object is to make bands, or hay-ropes, to tie up his trusses with. This operation is a curious and dexterous one. A boy holds a sort of winch, made of a string-bow, one end of which he turns in a socket of wood against his chest, by a swift motion of the hand.

The other end of the bow has a sort of hook, over which the man doubles a small bundle of the wetted hay. As this is turned round, it is twisted in his hand, and would form a rope only a few inches long, if he did not briskly supply the receding end with fresh parcels of hay from the heap. The boy steps backward, as the band lengthens; and, when at the distance of about three yards, it is detached, and another is as speedily prepared. Seventy-two of these bands—that being the number for a load of hay—have been made thus, by a man and boy, in twenty minutes; but half an hour is not too much for the work.

And now the cutter takes up his knife, consisting of a broad blade, about two feet long, with a handle standing square with the upper end. He thrusts this in where his cut begins, and, sawing it up and down, soon detaches a square corner. He then strikes into the parcel detached, a large two-tined fork, of which the prongs are about a foot long, and, thrusting his hand in at about the same distance down the side, he brings off a compact bundle of the hay, nearly square and flat; the external rough parts having been previously removed. This bundle is laid across two of the bands, which are then brought round, and twisted into a tight knot, with considerable strength and exertion. Hay-binders can usually guess within a pound the weight of a truss, which should be, if cut before Michaelmas, sixty pounds, if after, fifty-six pounds. But they do not trust to guessing. Steel-yards are always used, hooked on the shaft of a hay-fork, which two men support on their shoulders; and the weight must be accurately adjusted, or it will not be admitted to the market.

Thirty-six trusses constitute what is called a load of hay, in the south and eastern parts of England. In some parts a ton, or twenty hundred weight, is the quantity.

The manner in which hay is disposed of by the farmer, who sends it to London, is usually this: there are persons at the markets, called *salesmen*, who receive it as it comes in, and, on the proper market days, treat with the various customers who resort thither to buy. They are then responsible to the farmer, for whom they thus transact on commission, for the money for which it is sold, reserving to themselves five shillings a load for their agency. In this way, the vast quantities of hay seen in Smithfield, Whitechapel, the Haymarket, and other parts of London, are rendered to the consumers of the metropolis; and so great is the supply, sometimes, that country-dealers can go

to town, buy, and carry it home, at a cheaper
rate than that at which they could obtain it
where it was grown. Potatoes, fruit, and cattle, are managed in a similar way.

When grass has been cut early, and the season holds fine, a second crop of hay, usually
called *rowen*, may be obtained by the end of
August. But as this after-crop exhausts the
sward and soil very much, landlords seldom
allow it to be done; and the chance of fine
weather is not such as to tempt the farmer
much to this line of conduct. This second
hay, being softer to the mouth than the other,
is preferred for cows, who often thrive very
well upon it.

158

THE GRAIN HARVEST.

I will now give some account of the grain harvest, premising, however, that this is usually a most joyful season in all the land, especially when the harvest proves rich, and the sun is fair. In nothing are we more dependent upon a kind Providence than in respect to grain. It is our chief support. When, therefore, God has brought the harvest to maturity—when the fields wave with their rich burdens, and the sun beams forth from behind the passing cloud, indicating propitious weather for the harvest—then, indeed, it is a time to be glad.

Wheat having a hard and stiffish stem, or straw, is usually *reaped,* or cut with an instrument called *a sickle.* Some cradle it for the sake of the straw, which is cut longer, by the scythe working nearer the ground, but this is generally a wasteful way.

The little finger of my left hand bears witness to the rash confidence of one, who, like many others, thought that wheat was easy enough to cut, and who did not know that fingers' ends were still more easily shorn by unpractised operators. I nearly lost an useful digit at the second joint, by an ill-aimed slashing stroke, one memorable harvest-day; for, taking a bundle of wheat in my grasp, I eagerly drew the blade too near under my finger, and paid a penalty in pain, and the subsequent inability to use it.

A sickle is made nearly. in the form of a half-oval, and has a toothed edge, like a fine saw. To perform properly with this, the reaper must stoop low, take a large bundle in his left hand, and cut accurately and vigorously with his right. A party of reapers thus employed, proceed in the same regular way as mowers. They leave the wheat in small bundles at first on the ground, and afterwards tie it up in sheaves. The bands they make for this purpose are formed by twisting two small parcels of the straw together at the ends, taking care that the ears are not damaged by the knot. These sheaves are generally set up on the butts, for the sake of drying with more ease.

The harvest, I will suppose, is general now; and we have one hundred acres down. We have been a good deal interrupted by showery weather; but I do not think the wheat is materially damaged. Our carting, however, has been delayed; for wheat housed or stacked wet, spoils fast.

Pitching of wheat, that is, heaving up the sheaves on a long fork into the wagon, is very hard work. He who receives and adjusts it, is not fond of an incautious hand to pitch; for if the fork be thrust forward, instead of being withdrawn, it is apt to wound the face of him who takes it. I knew one who lost an eye through such a circumstance.

And now the beer, or some other drink, flows copiously indeed. The heat is great, and the evaporation from the human frame, whilst employed at the same time in severe labour, is such as to require a great supply of drink. It was formerly the practice to drink ardent spirits, and I am sorry to say that the custom is still continued by many. Not a few farmers, however, have discarded them entirely, and substituted beer, ale, coffee, or milk and water; and where the experiment has been properly made, the work is better done, and the labourers are far more healthful and far more happy.

The harvest weeks are indeed a period of toil and solicitude, which none can understand so well as those whose essential interests are at stake therein. To those especially, who are in difficulties for money, and have, perhaps, borrowed for this occasion — the danger of ruin from weather-spoiled, or otherwise deficient crops, is an oppressing anxiety. As with hay, so with other produce, the crop, which by weather is reduced to half its value, costs, perhaps, twice as much in extra labour to get it up. Let those, therefore, who regard as a calamity a shower of rain on the day of a proposed excursion, think how slight their trouble really is, compared with that of the industrious struggling agriculturist, whose hopes and labours for a year are, perhaps, exchanged for disappointment and despair by the dripping season!

There is not so much to explain, with regard to the grain harvest, as there is in hay-making, for this reason; grain is merely cut, carted, and housed; whilst grass, as we have seen, undergoes a sort of manufacturing process, distinct from the operation of gathering it in as a crop.

It is well, indeed, that wheat, for instance, which is sometimes ten months upon the ground, does not require more than mere harvest labours, otherwise it would be too costly a commodity for common use.

THRESHING AND DRESSING GRAIN.

I PASS on now to the business which forms, generally, part of the winter employment of the prosperous farmer, but which immediately follows harvest, with the needy and embarrassed class. The process of separating the grain from the ear has been performed in various ways, in different times and countries. The eastern nations placed their corn in the circular track-way of their cattle, who were driven over it, round and round a post. This practice is adverted to in St. Paul's quotation from the Jewish law: "Thou shalt not muzzle the mouth of the ox which treadeth out the corn." Both in the United States and in Europe, threshing is the common mode: a tedious one, it seems, but, nevertheless, as good, perhaps, all things considered, as any other method that has been adopted.

The flail is a smooth, hard, and heavy club of wood, largest at its further end, and about a yard long, fastened by a leathern thong to a handle somewhat longer. The joint is so contrived, by means of a part that turns round, that the flail may have a sort of circular motion, as it is wielded by the thresher. Before he begins, he sweeps the barn-floor, and carefully mends and stops any holes that he may see. He then takes sheaves from the *bays,* or elsewhere, and untying them, spreads them regularly on each side with the ears towards the middle of the floor. When thus adjusted, *he* begins—or *they*—for sometimes three or four are employed at once—to beat the ears with

the flail, at every stroke of which the grain
flies out of the husk.

It is quite impossible to put the young read-
er in possession of this, or other manual arts,
in general, by mere words; nor will the continued sight of the operation give the notion
which is to be acquired by practice. The use
of the flail, apparently so easy to the mere
observer, seems almost impossible to those

who first take it in hand. Unless it descend horizontally, so as to touch the floor with its whole length, the shock to the hand and arm is intolerable, whilst the grain probably remains untouched. The danger, however, to by-standers, is still greater, as the peasant knows, who hands the instrument to an unpractised operator. He instantly skips out of the way, well knowing that the intended blow is far more likely to reach his head than the grain below. One or two thumps generally suffice to cure the young beginner of any notions of his capability for that employment. He walks off, blowing his fingers, and not much comforted by the broad grin of the rustics in the barn.

When a sufficient quantity is threshed out, and the straw raked off, the process of dressing commences; that is, separating the grain from the chaff, small seeds, and refuse which is then amongst it. For this purpose, various methods have been adopted. Generally, those particles being lighter in proportion to their bulk than the grain, winnowing, or *winding*, will accomplish the purpose. This may be performed either by fanning with a large expanded machine of basket-work, or by setting the barn-doors open in an airy day, and then throwing the grain from a wooden shovel, a few yards, against the windy current. I have much admired the dexterity and success with which this has been done. The grain falls in one heap, and the chaff and rubbish in another, with astonishing precision.

But machinery has of late years superseded much of this skill and labour. These engines, by the strength of horses and mill-work, which we cannot here explain, will dispose of the winter's employment for several men, in a few

P

weeks, or, perhaps, days. Yet it is doubtful, seeing they are expensive, and subject to mismanagement and injury, whether the farmer gains much by them, beyond the mere convenience of a speedy preparation of his corn for sale.

Dressing machines, for cleansing the grain from chaff, &c. seem liable to fewer objections, and are very generally adopted now. The wind in these is occasioned by the rapid motion of wings, or flies, fixed on a revolving rod. A jolting motion is at the same time given to a wire sieve, down which the grain slides, and, in passing, the smaller seeds and particles are bolted through.

The next thing is to measure the grain into sacks for the market, or the miller;—much nicety, as well as honesty, is required here. The miller measures when he receives; and if there be half a pint deficiency he complains, and must have it rectified. Wooden bushels, of exact dimensions, are used. The top is struck off level, with a straight edge. Four bushels make a sack, eight bushels a quarter, and forty bushels one load of wheat.

The mode of threshing, dressing, and measuring other grain, seeds, and pulse, does not

COUNTRY MARKET.

differ enough to make a separate explanation
necessary.   In all cases it is required to have
the commodity as clean and free from mixture
as possible.

The farmer disposes of his grain generally,
by attending the neighbouring weekly markets, to which millers and corn-dealers resort;
or he sends it to Boston or New-York factors,
or sells to regular customers by private con-
tract.   Samples are usually taken to market
and elsewhere, in canvas bags; and on these,
bargains are made to a large amount.   I see
the miller in the engraving stands rather back,
as if in doubt.   Those, however, who do not
understand grain, would derive little knowledge
of the actual quality and value from the speci-
mens or the lump.   Persons are not unfre-
quently to be seen, and laughed at, who ex-
amine the samples, and talk about them, with

evidently no experience or real information on the subject. This is often observed in citizens, or mechanics, who have been known, with most consequential airs, to order *a quarter!* instead of a *quartern* of corn for a horse at an inn, pouring the grain from hand to hand at the same time, with the vain attempt to show how much they are *up* to "those fellows, the ostlers."

The public would get grain much cheaper than they do, were it not for the interference and rapacity of grain-factors and dealers, who step between the farmer and the miller, and merely buy to sell again. Of course, all that they gain, the public lose; but this might be borne, if they would not employ their money as they commonly do, to buy up or monopolize the supply, so as to put almost their own price upon it.

CORN MILL.

Millers are frequently dealers in this way, and make large sums, not only for their trouble of grinding and cleansing the meal, but by watching the markets, and buying and selling, as opportunities for making large profits may arise.

Perhaps my young readers will understand better a process of grinding grain adopted in England, by an examination of the engraving here given. We see here the part of the mill in which the grain is broken. It runs in from the wooden funnel, between the two stones; the upper one circulates with amazing rapidity. The stones being furrowed, or ground, bruise the corn as it flies towards the circumference. There it issues, and is afterwards cleansed from the chaff in other parts of the mill.

THE POTATOE CROPS.

THE potatoe is one of the most important vegetables raised in the United States. It is a native of South-America, whence it was carried to Spain from the neighbourhood of Quito. To England, however, this root found its way by a different route, being brought from Virginia by the colonists sent out by Sir Walter Raleigh, in 1586. It is now extensively cultivated in all the northern parts of the United States, and forms one of our principal articles of vegetable food.

Potatoes are raised with great ease, several hundred bushels being often produced on a single acre. Yet he that would have a large

crop must select a rich soil. The best potatoes generally grow on a dry and loamy soil,
provided the climate is a moist one; but if
the climate be dry, the soil may be strong and
heavy.

Potatoe grounds are sometimes ploughed up,
when the roots are ready, by which means
they are uncovered in a very speedy way for
the pickers. But this method cuts a great
many, and perhaps leaves many more in the
soil. A better method is to turn them out with
a flat three-pronged fork, made on purpose;
pickers following, with bags, or baskets, close
behind.

These roots *we* generally sort in the field—
the largest and best being reserved for the
table or for market—the smaller ones to feed
cattle and sheep. In England, farmers usu-
ually divide their potatoes into three sorts,

namely, *ware*, *middlings*, and *chats*. In the first class are put the very best, as to size, shape, and quality. They must not be the very largest, which do not sell well; not those of double form, or covered with protuberances, which are also rejected; and not any that are cut, or green, or hollow. The *middlings* are those of which the size is less than that esteemed the best. The *chats* are the smallest, the damaged, the discoloured; in fact, the refuse, designed for cows and hogs. These sell at about a third of the price of the best. The grower is obliged to give many pounds weight extra, into every hundred weight, to compensate the buyer for the weight of soil and sack in the scales. The profit of green-grocers in London and the suburbs, who sell potatoes retail by the pound to families, is enormous. They purchase them at the markets for three

or four pounds per ton, and sell them again at
a penny or five farthings a pound; by which
means their three or four pounds will bring
them in, not less than nine or ten guineas!
This could not be the case, if the London
public would take the trouble of sending to the
market for the commodity. As it is, the price
obtained by the grower seldom affords him a
fair profit, unless his land suit them uncom-
monly well, and the facilities be great of pro-
curing requisite manure.

TURNIPS.

TURNIPS, also, **are** raised in large quantities by some of the American farmers. They are less nutritious than the potatoe; but are useful for cattle and sheep during the winter season, while they are deprived of green vegetable food. Some farmers even fatten their cattle upon them. If cows are allowed to eat them, hot water must be added to their milk, or it will imbibe an unpleasant taste.

Turnips are very easily raised. The best method of obtaining a large crop is to turn over a piece of newly mowed sward land, rich and mellow; which having done, roll it with a heavy roller; then harrow it lightly; next, sow the seed, one thimble full, and only one, to a

square rod; bush it, roll it, and nothing further is needful, except to scatter ashes plen-
tifully upon the young plants, when they have
made their appearance. This should be done
just before a shower of rain.

GRASS.

WHEN land which has been under tillage is to be converted into pasture, some skill is required to select such species of grasses in due proportions, as may be best suited to the soil, and consequently afford the greatest quantity of produce during the year. The farmer knows from observation, that nature has provided, in all permanent pastures, a mixture of various grasses, the produce of which differs at different seasons; and his object should be to imitate nature in this department of his business. Many of my city friends, when on a visit in the country, have thought the blades of grass, constituting the sward under their feet, to be so nearly alike, as not to require the particular attention of the agriculturist. Now, I believe I may say, there are two hundred distinct kinds of grasses which will grow in this country, and which, separately, are of little value, yet collectively, and by judiciously combining the species appropriate to each soil, they form our richest pastures, and compose the sward, which is in the aggregate termed grass. The farmer's experience enables him to select the kinds of grass proper to form a close pasture for sheep, or deeper grazing for cattle or a meadow. I have endeavoured to give a description, with accompanying cuts, of a few only of the many species of plants, which are grown as herbage for cattle, more clearly to shew you how very distinct their form and appearance are upon a close examination.

1. The *Fox-tail* grass. This is a kind of grass which has a short bushy head, much like

a fox's tail. It is well suited to sheep and horses —but cows and hogs are not fond of it. It makes excellent hay.

FOX-TAIL GRASS.   SPIKED FESCUE GRASS.

2. The *Spiked fescue* grass. This grass is among the best for hay or pasture. It grows very luxuriant and productive, but is rather

Q

coarse. In one important particular it differs from most other grasses — it improves in proportion to its age.

FIORIN GRASS.

CAT'S-TAIL GRASS.

3. The *Fiorin* grass. This grass has been said to be a native of Ireland; but it has likewise been found growing spontaneously in this

country. It is much cultivated in England, and has been known to yield nine tons to the acre, in a season. Given to cows, it increases the quantity and improves the quality of milk.

4. *Cat's-tail* or *Timothy* grass. This grass is a native of the United States. It is sometimes called Cat's-tail from the resemblance of its head to the tail of a cat. It often goes by the name of *Herd's* grass, and is, perhaps, better known in New-England by this than any other name. It is said that it was first found in a swamp in Piscataqua, (Portsmouth, New-Hampshire,) by one Herd, who propagated it. It is the best of all our grasses. It often yields two or three tons of good hay to the acre, and thirty or forty bushels of seed. This grass was unknown in England until 1780, when it was taken thither by one Hudson.

HERBAGE PLANTS.

Clover. The cultivation of clover, and other herbage plants, is indispensable in the management of an arable or grain farm. Upon land which is not so rich as to allow of being constantly under tillage, but requires what we may term *rest,* by being for a short interval in pasturage, Clover, Lucern, Saintfoin, &c. are plants which the farmer finds greatly to his interest to cultivate. The clover family is numerous.

I give you a representation of two sorts, *Meadow Clover,* and *White Clover.* Meadow clover resembles red clover, which I have not described in this little work, but it is of a paler hue, not so high in its growth, with whitish flowers; it is a perennial plant, that is, continues to grow for a number of years. The red clover, which I allude to, only lasts two years.

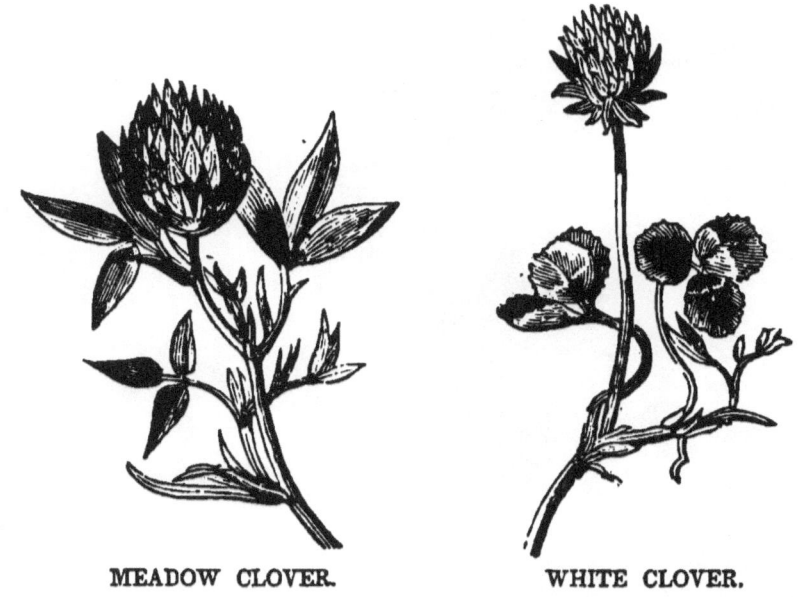

MEADOW CLOVER.   WHITE CLOVER.

White clover is also a perennial, and is often found in abundance in native pastures.

Lucern is a perennial plant, with clover-like shoots, the flowers blue or violet: it is not much recommended by farmers, who

LUCERN.

have tried it, for general culture, as it requires labour to keep it from grass and weeds.

Saintfoin is a perennial plant, with showy red flowers. It is a native of England, on dry, chalky soils. Its peculiar value is, that it will

SAINTFOIN.

grow on poor soils unfit for tillage. Its herbage is good for pasturage or hay, and it is generally considered a most valuable plant.

DEALING AND MONEY MATTERS.

And now, as we farmers, hearty and hungry as we are, by reason of our rural labours, do not grow *all* this corn and cattle for our own eating, it remains to shew in what way we gain or lose by the disposal of the produce, or by our various receipts and payments.

Farming, considered as a trade in commodities, *has* been a business wherein a man, of moderate means and capacity, might, with industry, get wealth. At present, those are reckoned prosperous farmers who manage to retain their property undiminished, and keep out of debt.

In this country, the farmers, as a class, are in a far happier condition than those in England. Here a majority of them are the owners of the soil which they cultivate—but in that country the land belongs chiefly to the great and powerful, called the nobility. Besides, we have in the United States but few taxes, and those, in comparison with the English farmer's taxes, are light and trivial. I will give some account of these matters in England, from which I am sure our little readers will readily perceive how much better the condition of the American farmer is than that of the English farmer. Observe, then, with whom the latter has to settle before he can count upon any profit from his toil. These are chiefly the King, the landlord, the clergyman, the overseer, the labourer, and those of whom

13   R

he purchases his stock, materials, and implements.

·The King's taxes are not what they used to
be: for, at one time, even agricultural horses, ·
and some kinds of carts, paid duty. The
chief thing remaining now, is the *land*-tax.

The landlord, as proprietor of the soil, has
an undoubted right to put any price he may
think proper upon it. It is for the farmer
to consider, before the bargain is made, what it
will suit him to give, taking other expenses into
the account. I may say, in a rough way, that
land, in England, varies from one pound, to two
or three pounds an acre, according to circumstances of soil, situation, and other particulars.

The rent and other matters being agreed
on, a written engagement for a term of years,
which binds the landlord to let, and the tenant

to hold, on certain conditions, is drawn up by a lawyer. This, I suppose, I need not say, is called *a lease.* The conditions are called *covenants,* in which the landlord is naturally disposed to take sufficient care of himself. Without going too much into dry matters, I will just say, that the principal covenant on the landlord's part is, to let the tenant have unmolested possession of the farm during the term granted; and this is an engagement from which he can in no way free himself; even though another should offer him ten times the rent.

The conditions on the part of the tenant are many, and sometimes grievous; yet such as men will consent to, for the sake of obtaining what they are apt to think, at first, will be a good business. He agrees to give so much money per annum, in quarterly payments;—he undertakes to farm the land in a certain way; — to keep the house and buildings in repair; — to manure to a certain extent; — to pay a heavy penalty, if he shall break up a pasture without leave. He engages, generally, not to cut the grass a second time in the season. Sometimes he is restricted from growing potatoes and from selling hay. He is forbidden to cut down the smallest timber tree. Sometimes the lease gives extra powers to the landlord, of raising rent, and enforcing penalties.

And suppose the farmer cannot pay his rent on the rent-day? The landlord then may distrain for it; that is, he can put a bailiff, a kind of constable, on the premises, and, after five days, he can seize any part of the property, and sell it, to pay himself. The worst of it s, that he can also seize and sell the property

of any other person which happens to be on
the spot at the time. I have heard an amusing
story of a certain squire, who sent a bailiff to
distrain for rent: the bailiff, looking over the
fields, espied a remarkably fine parcel of black
cattle, which he seized upon and sold without
inquiry. It happened, however, that these
were the landlord's *own beasts*, which had
accidentally strayed in!

The clergyman comes next; his claims are
called *tithes*, or *tenths*. The case is this: the
Church of England being by law established,
it became necessary to appoint and support its
ministers. Custom and law have, for many
ages, given a tenth part of the produce of the
land to the clergy, for the performance of
their duties. This portion they may take
either *in kind*, that is, the tenth sheaf of corn,

the tenth calf and lamb, the tenth measure of
milk, the tenth egg; or they may agree to
an equivalent, or *composition*, which perhaps
amounts to five or six shillings an acre. This
method is usual, and saves some trouble to
the parties concerned, and perhaps, too, some
strife.

The overseers are parish officers, whose
business it is to collect and lay out the *rates*,
or monies levied for the support of the poor.
These vary in amount, according to circumstances. Sometimes they are equal to a fourth,
sometimes to three-fourths of the whole rent;
so that a farmer who pays the landlord four
hundred pounds a year, may have to find also
one hundred and fifty pounds for the clergyman, and one, two, or three hundred for the poor
—those only (it should be) who are unable, by

their labour, to support themselves on their wages. This brings us to another branch of his expenditure.

The wages of men cannot long be fixed; they depend on the season of the year—the demand for labour—the price of grain, and the kind of employment. I think I may say that a person who farms four hundred acres, will have ten or a dozen men to pay on the Saturday night, at the rate of perhaps from ten to fourteen shillings a-piece. The man in the print does not look as if he were receiving less than he had fairly earned.

With regard to the purchase of stock and materials; the charge for machines and implements; carpenters', builders', wheelers', and blacksmiths' bills; the cost, or worth of his own produce for the cattle and horses, which

LABORERS RECEIVING THEIR WAGES.

he is obliged to keep; we cannot state particular sums. All I can say is, that these payments, added to rent, rates, and taxes, are such as to make farming, now that only a comparatively low price can be obtained for the produce, at best a hazardous, and, in many cases, a ruinous concern.

But let the times be what they may, the farmer can never succeed who has not judgment, industry, experience, and perseverance. His payments must be heavy; and they will exceed his receipts, if he makes a bad bargain with his landlord, mismanages and neglects his land, and buys and sells imprudently. Before he can deal to advantage, he ought to know well, and judge accurately of the real quality and value of the commodity, according to the markets. He ought to understand something of many trades connected with his own — as those of the miller, the salesman, the butcher, the grazier, the cattle and horse dealer — the land-agent, the builder, and even the lawyer, as far as his kind of property is concerned. He who is thus qualified, has talents and knowledge, which would make a man respectable, and most likely successful, in any other sphere or profession.

But the farmer is subject to numerous misfortunes, which none can prevent or foresee: bad seasons; blight and mildew; diseases in cattle; sudden falls in the value of produce; and various other casualties. A few of these circumstances occurring together, may reduce his profits to nothing, and compel him to waste his capital; and when that is gone, to trade with other men's money; so that, at last, he may sink to ruin.

But, although thus exposed to misfortune, the farmer has great reason to trust a kind Providence, which has promised that seed time and harvest shall not fail. In nearly every country on the globe there are times when farmers suffer in common with other classes of society; but after all, in a course of years, no other class perhaps is more smiled upon — none are more independent — none more happy. In England, it is true, the farmers have a hard time of it, as the saying is, but they may escape from some of their burdens by and by. Here, in the United States, we have much to encourage us — generally good crops — a fair market — light taxes — and, more than all, liberty to work or play as we please. Leaving others to follow what profession they please, we shall still cling to the honourable society of the farmers, and still say,

SPEED THE PLOUGH.

www.ingramcontent.com/pod-product-compliance
Lightning Source LLC
Chambersburg PA
CBHW030538040726
47497CB00008B/2506